AF281125

Dedicated to my family
and my home village

What is not fiction in this story may or may not be true. In the Finnish region of Savo, where most of the adventures of the Lava Prince take place, interpretation is left to the reader's and listener's discretion.

This English edition is based on the Finnish original Laavaprinssin salaisuus. Translated with DeepL Translator and DeepL Write.

Any resemblance to actual persons, living or dead, or to real companies or institutions, is purely coincidental. In particular, the character of the lady of the manor, Irma Arkko, is entirely fictional and serves as a contrast to the kind-hearted maid, Alma. In reality, the lady of the manor was an admirable, hardworking, and compassionate woman.

Arvola is a small rural village in southern Finland. At first glance, it appears quite ordinary—much like Tuomas, the half-orphan who lives on the Arkko estate. But Tuomas is haunted by a dark past that keeps him from living the life of a typical schoolboy.

The author dedicates this story to her home village, to which she would have wished a more prosperous and independent future.

Leena Pulfer

Leena Pulfer

The secret of the lava prince

Volume 1

© Copyright 2025 by Leena Pulfer

Cover: Dahlia D'Agosta

ISBN: 9 78-3-8192-1195-9

Publisher: BoD · Books on Demand GmbH,
Überseering 33, 22297 Hamburg,
bod@bod.de

Print: Libri Plureos GmbH,
Friedensallee 273, 22763 Hamburg

Table of Contents

Finally, the
ruler of the lava streams spoke:

Choose wisely, young prince:
Do you want to join the humans, that inferior
species that lives a short, meaningless life on
Earth, destroys everything around them
through their own stupidity, and turns to
dust when they die?
Or you can join your own lava people, who
have existed since the beginning of time and
cannot be destroyed by anything.
We can live on the earth and in its depths.
We can take any form we wish.
We have infinite powers.
Choose wisely.

1

At the start of science class, Ms. Paula Puntanen stood at the front of the room and asked, "Who saw the news about the volcanic eruption in Indonesia last night?"
Several hands shut up into the air.

"Who remembers the name of the volcano?" she continued.

The students glanced around uncertainly. A few shrugged. They shook their heads.

"No wonder none of you remember—it was Anak Krakatau. Volcanoes often have strange names given by locals. 'Anak Krakatau' means 'child of Krakatau.' Krakatau is the name of the volcanic island. But there are volcanoes in Europe with simpler names. Can anyone name one?"

More hands went up.

"Tuomas?"

"Etna," Tuomas said without hesitation. "It's in Sicily."

"I was just about to ask that—thank you, Tuomas."

Tuomas sank into his seat, annoyed with himself. Again, he'd answered too soon, before the teacher had even finished the question. He couldn't help it. With a bit of focus, reading people's thoughts was second nature to him. Perfectly normal... wasn't it?

Luckily, no one laughed. Ms. Puntanen smoothly launched into a story about her sister's recent trip to Sicily. "She was on a guided tour when Etna suddenly erupted," she said. "They had to scramble back to the hotel by bus, and even the airport shut down. Her flight was delayed for days."

She showed videos her sister had recorded. During the day, thick ash clouds billowed into a clear blue sky. At night, fiery streams shot from the crater like fireworks, illuminating the darkness in bursts of red and orange.

"Long ago, the locals believed gods lived inside the volcano," Ms. Puntanen said. "When the gods got angry, the mountain would erupt. These days, of course, we understand the science behind it. And that's our topic for today—volcanoes. You'll be working in groups."

Before splitting the class, she added, "But first, let me tell you a bit about Sicily's history. Did you know the island has been inhabited for over 5,000 years? It's been conquered by the Greeks, Romans, Vandals, and Spaniards."

She paused. "What else do you know about Sicily? Miranda?"

The blonde girl in the front row raised her hand. "There's the Mafia... and blood feuds."

Before Ms. Puntanen could respond, Mirko leapt to his feet. He crouched as if holding an invisible machine gun, spun in place, and fired off a stream of noises: "Pa-pa-pa-pa-pa-pa-pa!"

He brandished a ruler like a weapon, spraying spit as he spoke through the cleft in his palate.

"That's how they shot all their enemies! I saw it on TV!" he announced, standing tall and proud.

"Mirko!" Ms. Puntanen's voice snapped. "Sit down! Shooting people is not a game."

"I didn't shoot anyone. But Mafia bosses really do. They're not even scared of the police."

"Fortunately, things are different here in Finland. Now everyone calm down and get to work."

She divided the students into groups of four or five. Desks screeched across the floor as students dragged them together. Each group was to research how volcanoes form and what happens during an eruption.

Tuomas was grouped with Miranda, Väinö, and Mirko. They chose to focus on Mount Etna, since the teacher had just talked about it.

The classroom buzzed with energy. The topic fascinated everyone. None of the students had ever seen a volcano in real life—Finland had none.

"Mount Etna is the largest active volcano in Europe. It's on the Italian island of Sicily, in southern Europe..." Miranda typed the boys' words on her laptop. Though blind, she worked swiftly with her Braille keyboard, which simultaneously displayed the text in standard print.

"What does it look like when a volcano erupts?" she asked.

"I've got some pictures... oh, right," Väinö said, catching himself.

"Clouds of ash and smoke rise from the top of the mountain," Mirko described.

"What kind of smoke? I only know the smell from heating the sauna."

"It's soft... like cotton," Tuomas offered, hesitating. He found it difficult to imagine how Miranda experienced the world—no colors, no shapes, no sense of distance. Not even a reflection. She didn't know that she was beautiful. Words like "beautiful" or "ugly" meant nothing to her.

"It'd be exciting to live in a place like that," Mirko said dreamily. "Like living next to a nuclear plant—you never know when it might blow."

"But not so exciting for the people who lose their homes... or their lives," Väinö replied. He was the opposite of Mirko: quiet, thoughtful, and built like a sumo wrestler—just half a meter shorter than his father.

Mirko read aloud from his tablet:

"The lava is bright red when it reaches the surface and over a thousand degrees Celsius. It moves like a sprinter. As it cools, it turns dark red, hardens, and slows. The lava burns everything it touches—trees, wooden houses. Only stone walls or churches might survive. The solidified lava and rock fragments crush everything in their path."

"That's awful," Miranda whispered.

"Good thing we don't have volcanoes here in Finland," Tuomas said quietly.

He had no idea that his roots stretched far beyond Finland—all the way to Sicily. Or more precisely, into the fiery heart of Mount Etna itself.

2

*The story about Tuomas' grandparents
begins in the first half
of the last century.*

Tuomas had believed that his grandparents had spent their entire lives on the Costa family estate on the Italian mainland. Nonna had never mentioned that her roots were on the island of Sicily. She had good reason to keep this secret.

3

The people living near Mount Etna were used to tremors and lava flows. They carried on with their lives, setting toppled knickknacks back on shelves, rinsing gray ash from garden leaves, and wiping a fine dusting from patio tables.

No one expected a major eruption, even though the earth had been trembling more violently than usual for weeks, and plumes of smoke curled steadily from the crater into the blue sky. When stronger quakes rattled the soles of their feet and sent pans clattering in kitchens, people crossed themselves instinctively. Even the 6 a.m. Mass was full —packed with villagers Father Anthony hadn't seen in years.

Still, no one was truly alarmed. The volcano had erupted many times in living memory, and records showed it had done so for centuries before. Even during the worst of it, the valley had suffered only from ash. It darkened the skies for weeks before settling on the roofs of whitewashed houses, cobbled streets, winding paths, cars, and gardens. Breathing was difficult—the ash carried tiny glass shards from the molten rock within the crater.

The villagers knew what to do. They swept the ash from the streets, carted it to the village edges, or heaped it at the borders of gardens. Men cleared rooftops and car; women wiped down windows again and again. On days like those, no one dared hang laundry out to dry on the lines strung between the houses.

But when the heavy rains finally came, they washed the ash from the streets. Leaves turned green again. Flowers and grass pushed through the dust. The cattle, long fed on dry fodder, returned to grazing. Broken roof tiles were replaced, fallen crosses and Madonna portraits were rehung. Life returned to normal, as if nothing had happened.

This time was different.

The volcano erupted in the dead of night. A deafening boom and a massive quake tore through the town, jolting everyone from their beds. Villagers poured into the streets, which felt safer than the crumbling houses. Despite the fear, they couldn't look away from the mountain's fiery spectacle: jets of fire burst from the crater into the dark sky, casting an eerie glow through clouds of ash.

The ground shook and groaned beneath their bare feet. Children and teens, who had never seen such a violent eruption, screamed and laughed with excitement as more explosions echoed down the valley, flinging fireballs for miles. Only the youngest ran crying into the arms of their mothers and grandmothers.

Old Ettore, the local poacher, stepped out onto the road, binoculars in hand. He lived at the edge of town in his brother's house and usually used those binoculars to hunt rabbits and birds on the volcano's slopes. His old hunting dog, Bono—a slender, long-legged Sicilian greyhound—growled softly, on edge from the chaos.

Ettore scanned the mountainside, lit in shades of red and gold by the volcanic glow. His breath caught.

"Lava! Lava's coming down the slope!"

"Don't talk nonsense, you forest thief," muttered the man beside him, grabbing the binoculars and raising them to his eyes. But a moment later, he gasped. "Porca miseria! The man's right! It's flowing into the valley!"

The binoculars passed from hand to hand. Murmurs grew into shouts.

"The lava is coming!"

And it was. A wide fissure had opened in the volcano's flank. Molten lava gushed through the crack, streaming toward the valley—and straight for the town of Mascali.

In the past, lava had always flowed from the main crater and made its way down the far side of the mountain, eventually reaching the sea, where it cooled into thick, black rock along the shore.

But now, the villagers stood frozen, like spectators at a theater, waiting for the next act. The crater spewed more fountains of fire. Huge boulders exploded from the peak, crashing down the dark slope and settling, as if waiting for the lava to resume their journey.

As the night dragged on, the river of fire widened. No one knew how long it would last. How fast it would move. Whether it would reach the hillside farms, the scattered cottages—and eventually, the valley towns.

"Run, Aldo! Tell the to ring the bells!" Ettore shouted to his open-mouthed nephew. "It could be dangerous!"

"Nonna, are we all going to die?" little Livia whimpered from her grandmother's lap, having overheard Ettore's cry.

"Don't be afraid, bambina. The Lord of the Volcano is angry now, but he will calm down if we pray with all our hearts."

Soon, the bell tower rang out through the darkness, summoning the faithful. The church quickly filled. Father Anthony offered comfort in the name of all the saints and the Virgin Mary. His appearance—a nightcap askew on his head and his housekeeper's silk robe tied loosely at the waist—might have invited laughter on another night. But no one laughed.

The village police chief, the fire chief, and the Commissario di Polizia were there too. After Mass, they huddled with Father Anthony in the sacristy.

They agreed: better to wait for dawn. Perhaps the lava would stop. Perhaps it would veer away from town. After all, the prayers had been fervent.

Candles flickered before the altar. More than a few villagers dropped coins in the collection box—perhaps spurred by sudden piety, or perhaps by the presence of the police chief. In any case, they had done their part. The rest was in God's hands.

The authorities decided not to issue an evacuation order—yet. If the lava kept moving, it would still take days to reach the city. Their choice to wait was, at least for now, understandable.

That night, only the very young and the elderly remained inside. Everyone else kept watch from the streets and fields. At first, they needed binoculars to see the lava's progress. But before long, it glowed clearly even to the naked eye.

Cheers rose when the lava seemed to stop behind a massive boulder—only to die away in stunned silence when it split and flowed around the rock in twin rivers of fire. The two lines merged once more into a single, unstoppable stream, creeping steadily down the slope toward their town.

4

The walls—and even the roof—of the Costa family's modest home were built from gray slate quarried long ago from the volcano itself. From a distance, the house blended almost seamlessly into the barren mountainside. At one end of the building, a simple stable sheltered a few goats and chickens. Just beyond a thin partition, Father Luigi and his grown son, Maurizio, had carved out a small kitchen and a bare-bones bedroom.

For the past three months, Mother Giulia had been in a hospital in Catania, twenty kilometers away. Any hope of a cure had long since vanished. The cancer had spread too far, and surgery wasn't just futile—it was also unaffordable. Luigi and Maurizio took turns visiting her, gently urging her to eat, bringing her bunches of muscatel-scented grapes that clung to the stone walls of their home.

The night before the eruption, after another heavy-hearted visit to the hospital, Maurizio had stopped at a trattoria for a few glasses of vino rosso before pedaling his old bicycle back to the valley. At home, Luigi had found comfort at the bottom of a wine bottle. Not stopping at a glass, he drank the whole thing and eventually passed out on the warm stone bench against the wall of the house.

Bruno, the family's old sheepdog, had been restless all evening. He lay beside Luigi's feet, whining and twitching. Finally fed up, Luigi dragged himself up and locked the dog in the shed with the goats and chickens. But Bruno was clever and knew how to open the latch. So Luigi chained him to the wall.

Higher up the mountainside lived Nino, the shepherd, in a hut he shared with a dozen sheep. For days, Nino had felt the ground shifting uneasily beneath his boots. He'd felt it before. But this time was different. The distant booms confirmed his unease, and when he looked toward the summit, his heart jumped. Fire burst from the crater, painting the sky blood-red. Ash clouds billowed upward like smoke from a war zone.

Nino couldn't yet see the lava, but he could hear it—trees cracking, rocks tumbling, the distant crash of earth splitting apart.

He jumped onto his small tractor. For a moment, he hesitated. Should he try to load the sheep onto the trailer? No. The animals were spooked and herding them now would take too long. The sounds from the hillside were growing louder—more urgent. Nino leapt down, flung the hut door open, and herded the sheep out as best he could. Then he fired up the engine.

His matted sheepdog, Husso, darted back and forth, torn between staying with the flock or following his master. At the last second, he chose the sheep.

The winding dirt road from Nino's hut led down toward the valley, past the Costa family's home. As he passed the gate, Nino hit the brakes.

"Luigi! Maurizio! Are you still home? You've got to come now!"

Bruno barked frantically from the shed. Nino jumped down, rushed to the front door, and pounded on it.

"Luigi! Maurizio! Are you asleep in this hellhole?"

Inside, Luigi groaned and sat up, rubbing his eyes. "Nino? What the hell are you doing here in the middle of the night?"

But when he looked past Nino toward the hillside, he saw it: a jagged red glow pulsing between the charred black tree trunks. Even in his fog of wine and sleep, Luigi understood. He had to move—now.

He scrambled onto the tractor behind Nino, and the two men rumbled down the path in the slow but steady machine. It would have been enough to carry them to safety—if fate hadn't intervened. A massive boulder, hurled from the crater, smashed into the road, striking the tractor and knocking it from the narrow track. Tractor and trailer tumbled down the slope, crashing through brush and stones before coming to rest in a twisted heap.

Luigi and Nino were both badly injured and unconscious. In a strange way, it was a mercy. Neither of them felt the searing heat creeping down the hillside as morning approached.

Bruno had broken free from his chain and managed to open the shed door. He sprinted after the tractor, his bark echoing in the night. When he reached the wreckage, he found his master lying motionless, his feet crushed beneath a wheel. The old dog circled the wreck, whining, then crawled beneath it. His chain, still dragging behind him, caught on the axle. Bruno pulled and twisted, but it was no use.

Realizing he couldn't escape, Bruno stopped struggling. He lay down beside Luigi, licked his face gently, and waited.

Farther down the road, the bleating of the terrified sheep echoed through the volcanic night. Husso, still leading the flock down toward the valley, suddenly halted. He had heard the faint, desperate barking of his old friend.

Turning, he spotted the tractor, barely visible in the shifting red light of the volcano.

Husso left the flock and ran to the wreck. He sniffed the wreckage, nuzzled Luigi's limp hand, then turned to Bruno. The old sheepdog's muzzle twitched, and he gave Husso a weak wag of his tail.

Husso licked Bruno's face once—softly—then turned back. There was nothing he could do.

With a final, sorrowful howl, the sheepdog returned to the road and trotted after the herd, disappearing into the ash-blurred shadows of the valley.

5

Maurizio woke on a park bench at dawn, coughing. The rough bark of a nearby tree scratched at his cheek, and a fine layer of ash coated his face, his coat, and the worn saddle of his bicycle leaning nearby.

He squinted against the strange light, trying to piece together the previous night. He'd left the trattoria later than planned—and after too much vino rosso, he'd made the mistake of chasing it with grappa. Still, he must have had the good sense not to bike home in that state. Instead, he'd collapsed on this bench, hoping to sleep off the worst of it. With his mother dying in the hospital, an accident—or worse, an arrest—would have been unthinkable.

But why was he coughing?

The air stung his throat and eyes. It wasn't the wine. It was ash.

Maurizio pulled his scarf up over his nose and mouth—the one he always wore into town—and climbed onto his bicycle, pedaling toward home.

Something was wrong.

The road leading out of Mascali was packed with people fleeing. Trucks rumbled by, piled high with furniture and frightened passengers. Overloaded cars honked and swerved. Tractors dragging trailers that looked like mobile homes trundled through the haze. Donkeys brayed as they pulled wagons, and men pushed handcarts heavy with blankets, boxes, and water jugs while children and women walked beside them.

At an intersection just outside town, a policeman stepped into Maurizio's path, rifle slung across his chest.

"Stop! Turn around! No one's allowed into town—"

"It's me, Maurizio," he said, pulling down his scarf.

The officer squinted through the ash. "Maurizio? Madonna mia. You scared me."

"Enrico?" Maurizio said, recognizing his old school friend. "What's going on? Why's everyone fleeing?"

Enrico didn't answer right away. He looked tired. Angry. Afraid.

"If the houses are empty," he finally said, "some people might loot."

"Loot? Why would the houses be empty?"

Enrico blinked at him. "Did you fall from the moon? The volcano's erupting. The lava's flowing down the southern slope—straight toward the town."

Maurizio felt cold, even in the thick, hot air. "I have to get home. My father—our animals—they need to be evacuated."

"I think it's too late." Enrico's voice softened. "The lava already passed your place. No one stayed behind—there was too much noise, too many warnings. I'm sure your father made it out. Check in town. He's probably at your aunt's."

Maurizio didn't stop in Mascali. He pedaled hard up the familiar road toward home. The ash in the air thickened with every turn. The heat became unbearable. Rounding a curve, he slammed on the brakes.

There it was.

The hillside was no longer a hillside. It was a rolling, glowing ocean of molten rock, cracked and steaming, alive with color and sound. Great blackened boulders drifted in the flow. Charred tree trunks bobbed in the current like fallen matchsticks. The edge of the lava advanced slowly, steadily, consuming everything in its path.

His family's slate-roofed house had been higher up the slope. Gone.

Maurizio turned his bicycle around and rode back into town, heart pounding with dread.

In Mascali, chaos reigned. Loudspeakers blared from a police cruiser inching through the narrow streets:

"There is no need to panic. The eruption will end soon. The city will be spared. Army trucks are on standby. Pack a few days' essentials. Lock your homes. Police will remain to prevent looting. There is no need to worry."

Maurizio didn't believe a word.

He headed for his aunt's house, where he hoped to find his father.

"Zia Teodora! Have you seen Papa?"

His aunt didn't even register the question. She paced wildly around her bedroom, muttering, "What should I take? What should I take?" Overturned suitcases lay open on the bed, surrounded by jewelry boxes, silverware, crystal glasses from her wedding (twelve), stacks of old photographs, albums, a black funeral suit, slippers, copper pots, porcelain figurines, hand-stitched cushions, religious icons—the Virgin Mary in a plastic frame, a gilded cross.

"Arrivederci, Zia Teodora," Maurizio said from the doorway.

She didn't even notice he was leaving.

In a neighboring courtyard, shouting and crying erupted. Maurizio peered over a low wall.

A little girl clung to a fat, brightly colored rabbit. Her father, bleeding from a nicked hand, tried to pry the rabbit from her arms by its ears.

"Balbina! Mama! Help me!" she sobbed.

"You can't take that thing with you, and we can't leave it here! We need meat for the road!" the man shouted.

The girl's mother didn't even look up. She was digging up potted flowers beside the house. Two buckets already brimmed with dirt and roots.

"Woman, are you insane? We're not bringing the plants!" the father roared.

The rabbit seized the opportunity, kicked free of the man's grasp, and bounded down the street, disappearing into the maze of alleyways.

Maurizio moved on. The streets were piled with mattresses, crates, and overloaded cars. He passed neighbors and called out, asking if anyone had seen his father. They barely looked at him. No one asked about his mother in the hospital, as they usually would have. Maybe his father had gone to Catania—maybe he was already at her bedside.

Then, something leapt at his bicycle, nearly knocking him off balance.

A dog.

Old Husso.

Maurizio blinked. "Husso? You're here?"

The dog barked once and wagged his tail—but his eyes were dull, frightened.

The sheep Husso had been guarding had made it to town, but the noise and crowds had panicked the flock. The animals had scattered, and Husso had failed to regroup them.

Maurizio knelt and stroked the dog's ragged fur. Hope stirred in his chest.

If Husso was here, then maybe Dino was too. And if Dino had come down from the mountain, surely he'd brought his friends—his father and Bruno.

"Where's Dino? Where's Bruno?" Maurizio whispered. "Find them, Husso. Go!"

Husso barked again, short and sad. Then he lay down, resting his head on his paws, eyes full of sorrow.

Maurizio understood. He'd worked with animals all his life. Husso didn't need to speak.

He climbed back on his bicycle.

Husso followed for a few steps, then stopped, turned back, and let out one long, mournful howl before vanishing down a side street.

Later, Maurizio would hear stories. In the narrow alleys, people had begun catching the scattered sheep. They lifted them onto tractor beds or pushed them into the arms of children sitting in cars. The meat would be valuable in the days ahead.

Some dogs—those without owners, those left behind— roamed the outskirts of town in confused packs. They howled at the red sky, as the lava crept closer and closer to the valley.

6

As the volcano finally quieted and the thick smoke began to lift, the air grew clearer, crisper. From a low-flying survey plane, the southern slope of Mount Etna came into view—blanketed in hardened lava and pale gray ash. The small town at the base of the mountain was barely recognizable, swallowed by a blackened tide. Fields, roads, homes—vanished beneath a scorched, undulating sea of rock.

Only one structure remained standing on the mountainside: a solitary gray stone house surrounded by a cluster of ancient olive trees. Their twisted limbs still reached toward the sky. Under the layers of ash clinging to the leaves, hints of pale green shimmered in defiance. All around them, charred stumps pierced the hardened flow like blackened bones.

The plane banked and circled once over the isolated property. No movement—no people, no animals. With no signs of life, the rescue team moved on.

When the lava finally cooled and the immediate danger had passed, Maurizio joined the returning evacuees to witness the aftermath. In the town, remnants of life remained—a stone church half-filled with cooled lava, rooftops peeking from under the hardened mass, the outlines of alleyways barely visible. The road that once connected the town to Maurizio's home had disappeared completely, swallowed by the flow.

He left his bicycle behind and began to cross the jagged lava field on foot. The sharp rock crunched under his boots. Landmarks he had known his entire life were gone:

trees, stone fences, stables—erased. Yet somehow, through instinct or memory, his feet found the way.

And then—he stopped.

There, in the distance, a patch of green emerged through the desolation. His breath caught in his throat.

The olive grove.

It wasn't a hallucination. It wasn't wishful thinking born of grief. The garden was still there, ringed by olive trees—scarred but standing. His family's house was intact.

He ran.

The lava had created a natural barricade of boulders and jagged rock, enclosing the house and garden on three sides. A towering, black wall of volcanic stone now stood where the vineyard once was. The only way to reach the house from the valley was to climb.

Maurizio stood at the edge of the garden, heart pounding.

Everything looked unchanged—and yet, everything had changed. Ash still blanketed the olive leaves, and a fine gray powder dulled the grass. But the silence… it was wrong. Too complete.

No bleating goats. No clucking chickens. No bark from Bruno. The bench by the wall was empty. The front door creaked softly in the breeze but remained closed.

Everyone was gone—his father, his mother, Bruno, the animals. Gone.

Maurizio sat on the bench—the one where he and his father used to drink wine at dusk, watching the valley bathe in golden light. Now the valley was buried, and his father… gone with it. His mother had passed, too—peacefully, in a coma on the night of the eruption. She had been spared the pain of knowing she'd lost everything.

Grief hollowed him out. He lowered his head into his hands, and the tears came fast and soundless.

Then... the front door creaked.

His head jerked up.

Standing in the doorway was someone in his mother's old work dress.

Maurizio's blood ran cold. No. She was gone. This isn't possible.

But before he could speak, the figure rushed forward and wrapped him in a desperate embrace.

"I thought everyone was dead—but you're alive!" a voice sobbed into his chest.

He pulled back, stunned. "Who... who are you?"

"I'm sorry," the girl said, stepping away. Her face was streaked with soot and tears. "I came here without permission. I didn't know where else to go. I'm... Olivia."

7

Olivia—if that was her name—couldn't tell Maurizio anything about herself. Not even later.

She remembered nothing. Not her family, not where she'd lived, not how she'd survived the eruption, or how she'd found her way to the Costa house. It was as if the lava had scorched not only the land but her entire past. All she could say was:

"Even my clothes were torn. I had to take something from the closet."

She said it softly, almost apologetically.

Maurizio didn't care. It didn't matter who she was or that she wore his mother's best Sunday dress. He had fallen for her the moment he saw her. She was unlike anyone he had ever met—graceful, radiant, with sapphire-blue eyes and a cascade of red curls that framed her delicate face like flames.

The house and garden had somehow survived the eruption, spared by a miracle. But they couldn't stay. Maurizio, honorable by nature, would not risk Olivia's reputation by spending the night alone with her under one roof.

So he packed a small rucksack with only the essentials: a change of clothes, the family savings, the household register, an envelope of his father's papers, and his mother's jewelry box—modest in value but too precious to abandon to looters. Before leaving, he carefully took down the picture of the Madonna his mother had prayed to daily and the wedding photo of his parents, their faces solemn and proud.

"We'll come back," Maurizio whispered to the house as he shut the door behind him.

It was a promise he intended to keep.

Together, they climbed down the valley, navigating the uneven lava fields. Under a ridge of twisted rock, Maurizio spotted the twisted metal frame of Dino's tractor seat protruding from the scorched mass. Of those who had once lived on the slope, nothing else remained.

The city of Catania was in chaos. Authorities scrambled to track who had died, who had fled, and who had simply vanished. Countless people had abandoned their homes in panic, leaving behind their identification and documents. Many couldn't even prove who they were.

Luckily, someone always stepped forward: a bar owner, a retired schoolteacher, or Father Antonio—each offering testimony that Maria Manzoni was indeed Maria Manzoni, and that Sergio Salvini had not assumed someone else's name.

Maurizio, more prepared than most, had brought his papers, including the family register that listed his parents and their wedding date. He and Olivia found Father Antonio, who had also fled to Catania, and asked him to marry them.

Since a funeral had to be held for Maurizio's mother, the two ceremonies were combined. The same friends, neighbors, and extended family would have attended both anyway. Olivia, it seemed, had no one of her own.

"What is your name, my daughter?" Father Antonio asked gently.

"Olivia," she whispered.

"And your last name?"

She looked down. Said nothing.

"You must remember your last name," he coaxed kindly.

"Olivia… Monti," Maurizio interjected, stepping in to protect her. The name had come to him in an instant. He had met her on the mountain—monte. It felt right. He invented the rest on the spot: her birthdate, her parents.

"Parents?" the priest asked gently.

"Dead to me," Olivia said, then lowered her face and began to sob.

Aunt Teodora had brought along her late husband's suit. It was pressed into service as Maurizio's wedding attire. Olivia wore the black mourning dress that had belonged to Maurizio's mother. No one knew the bride. As they entered the church, Maurizio noticed the sideways glances, the whispered suspicions. Some disapproved.

He didn't care. He placed his strong arm around Olivia's waist. This was his wife now—his treasure, his miracle from the mountain. He would protect her always.

But after the ceremony, a question hung in the air: Where would they go? How would they live?

Maurizio was strong, hard-working, and decent, but few could afford to pay builders to restore their ruined homes. Jobs were scarce. Rebuilding was slow.

It was even worse for Olivia. Despite her gentle manner and lowered eyes, despite the way her red hair was tucked beneath her headscarf, old women who came seeking housekeepers or kitchen help made the sign of the cross and muttered about the curse of the volcano. They slammed their doors in her face.

News of the eruption eventually reached the Italian mainland.

Pietro Costa, in the rolling hills of Tuscany, read the reports and thought of his distant cousin Luigi, who had lived near Etna. Had they survived? Had they lost everything? Would they come north?

Pietro's farm, La Colombaia, was in desperate need of help. The land was fertile, but he couldn't manage it alone.

He wrote a letter.

It passed from hand to hand, post office to church rectory, until it reached Maurizio in Catania. The offer came as a lifeline. Maurizio and Olivia accepted.

Maurizio's heart ached to leave Sicily—his birthplace, his past—but Olivia never looked back. She couldn't bear to. Her eyes avoided the volcano at every turn, her body stiffened whenever the wind carried the scent of ash.

"The mountain's calm now," Maurizio said one evening as they stood near the port.

Olivia didn't reply at first. Then, softly, she said:

"He'll never forget."

And she fell silent.

8

The story of Tuomas' grandparents continues

The La Colombaia estate—the dovecote—stood proudly on a lush green hill above the town of Marradi. The winery had been part of the landscape for centuries, a solid stone house built with slabs hauled by ox cart from a nearby quarry. Time had weathered its walls but not its dignity.

At the heart of the two-story structure rose a square tower with arched windows, each one designed with small openings for pigeons. The building had once accommodated a large family. The ground floor housed a cool wine cellar, storerooms, and a pigsty where broad-backed sows nursed squealing piglets.

Over the years, the Costa family had dwindled. By the time Mount Etna erupted, only the aging couple—Pietro and Agata Costa—and their two unmarried sons, Antonio and Giovanni, still lived there.

The arrival of a young relative from Sicily, with his quiet, red-haired wife, was a welcome surprise.

Olivia had no background in housekeeping, but she learned quickly and without complaint. Her presence brought warmth to the cold stone halls, and soon, the sound of children's laughter echoed through La Colombaia once more. First came Angela, then her brother Carlo. Both inherited their father's dark hair and brown eyes.

Pietro and Agata were overjoyed. For the first time in years, the future of the estate felt secure.

When Pietro fell ill, he transferred the winery to Maurizio. His sons Antonio and Giovanni were given the right to live on the property for the rest of their lives and were allotted several hectares of land.

Pietro passed away a year later, his heart finally giving out. Agata remained for many more years, becoming a loving, steady presence in the lives of her grandchildren.

Maurizio and Olivia thrived at La Colombaia. Here, Olivia's red hair—once met with suspicion and fear in Sicily—was accepted without comment. The village whispered no dark rumors. The shadows of her past seemed to lift.

But happiness, as always, proved fragile.

Like his mother Giulia, Maurizio was diagnosed with cancer. He fought hard but died at the age of fifty.

Olivia was devastated. Her once-bright eyes dulled. Her children, now grown, had long since left the nest. Angela had become a flight attendant and fallen in love with a Finnish pilot. Carlo worked as a chef in a hotel in Switzerland and had married a waitress named Sofia.

Now, the once-vibrant estate stood still again.

Olivia, bent with grief and age, wandered its halls like a ghost. Antonio and Giovanni, aging bachelors themselves, were in no condition to run a winery. And the question loomed over the hillside like a silent question mark:

Who would carry on the legacy of La Colombaia?

9

After their father's funeral, Carlo and Angela stayed on at La Colombaia for a few days to be with their mother. The house, once filled with life, felt quieter now, but not hopeless.

One afternoon, as the sunlight poured through the kitchen window, Carlo shared an idea.

"We should turn the winery into a restaurant," he said. "Sofia and I could come back. With my cooking and her experience managing a dining room, we could make it work."

Angela raised an eyebrow. "You really think so?"

Carlo nodded. "Antonio's wine, Giovanni's organic prosciutto, Mamma's pasta... come on. Locals would love it. Tourists, too."

Olivia's face lit up with cautious hope. Antonio and Giovanni, both long past their prime, gave tired but approving nods. Carlo's plan offered more than just a new business—it was a way to keep the family close.

Carlo and Sofia would return with their young daughter, Chiara. Angela and her Finnish-born son, Tuomas, could continue spending holidays at the estate. The old stone house, with its many rooms and thick walls, had more than enough space for everyone.

Renovations began almost immediately.

The 200-year-old building was transformed with care and creativity. The cramped storerooms were opened up to form a bright, spacious dining room with arched windows overlooking the vineyards. The kitchen was modernized without losing its rustic charm. Original beams remained exposed, and antique furniture was restored. After months of hard work, Ristorante La Colombaia opened its doors.

Tuomas, now a bright and curious boy, always looked forward to visiting Nonna Olivia. She spoiled him with hugs, sweet fruit, and bowls of fresh pasta. Despite Angela's bouts of homesickness for Finland, she and Tuomas traveled to Italy several times a year.

Now that his cousin Chiara—just his age—was living there, Tuomas had even more reason to love his visits. Thanks to his fluent Italian, he and Chiara became fast friends. They spent long summer afternoons chasing lizards through the olive groves, helping in the vineyard, or inventing elaborate stories beneath the dovecote tower.

La Colombaia had come back to life—stone by stone, recipe by recipe, memory by memory.

10

Another summer at La Colombaia had come to an end. Angela and her son, Tuomas, woke early to catch the morning flight from Florence to Helsinki. School would start again for Tuomas on Monday.

Outside, it was still dark. Rain lashed against the windows, but inside the kitchen, the fire in the stove glowed warmly. The house was quiet, wrapped in the scent of woodsmoke and espresso.

As always, Nonna Olivia had been up since before four, kneading pasta dough by hand. She had lovingly set the table for the departing travelers—fresh farmhouse bread, homemade honey, and cheese. The aroma of strong espresso filled the room.

Carlo sat calmly at the table, sipping his coffee, even as Angela urged him to hurry.

"Carlo, come on. We'll be late."

Angela, as usual, passed on the coffee. She drank a glass of fresh orange juice—caffeine made her jittery. Tuomas sat half-asleep in his chair, too tired to eat.

"Tommaso will have breakfast on the plane," Angela said, as Olivia tried to offer him a banana.

Carlo just smiled. "Subito, sorella mia. We'll make it in my car."

Nonna Olivia moved in front of Tuomas and gently stroked his red hair with her weathered hands.

"Mio caro Tommaso, how I wish I could keep you here," she murmured. "May Saint Christopher and all the saints protect you on your journey—and bring you back to me."

She took a thin gold chain from around her neck. A dark stone hung from it—polished smooth, almost glowing. She clasped it gently around Tuomas's neck and kissed him on both cheeks.

"Don't forget your Nonna."

"Oh, Mamma," Angela sighed, a little embarrassed. "We'll be back soon. The next holidays are just around the corner."

Tuomas blushed at the public affection, but didn't take off the necklace. He figured he could do that later. Still, he loved his grandmother nearly as much as he loved his own mother.

Finally, Carlo was ready. Despite the rain, the whole family gathered outside to say goodbye: Nonna Olivia, uncles Giovanni and Antonio, Carlo's wife Sofia. Little Chiara was still asleep.

Angela gave Tuomas her coat to use as a blanket in the back seat. The winding road from Marradi to Florence stretched ahead—fifty kilometers of twisting hills through Tuscany.

Carlo drove with ease. His new Porsche purred like a contented tiger. It wasn't the kind of car a village innkeeper could normally afford, but a wealthy guest from Florence—owner of a car import business—had taken a liking to Carlo and La Colombaia. After one especially joyful evening, he'd gifted Carlo the car as a token of friendship.

Tuomas had just drifted off to sleep when he half-heard his mother whisper to Carlo.

"Mom never took that necklace off. Not even at the beach. And she never gave it to me. Her only daughter."

"She's old," Carlo replied gently. "They all get a little strange when they're older... She just misses you. You could always stay here, you know. We've got plenty of room. We could run the restaurant together. Your husband could visit between flights."

Angela sighed. "You know I wouldn't last a week with Sofia. She's too opinionated—and so am I."

"Then that's that," Carlo said, shrugging. He turned up the radio and began whistling along, already daydreaming about a leisurely afternoon in Florence's cafés and boutiques. The family could handle lunch without him.

Then Angela's voice broke sharply through the music.

"Attenzione! Up ahead—Oh God—!"

A flatbed truck, unlit and broken down, loomed around the next curve, nearly invisible in the dark and rain. There was no time to brake. Carlo's Porsche slammed into it at full speed, the sleek front end crushed beneath the steel trailer.

The roof tore away.

The car disappeared into the black wall of metal.

The impact was instant. There was no time for anyone to scream.

Tuomas never fully woke. He was flung to the floor of the car, crushed beneath twisted seats and debris. Then, silence.

It was nearly an hour before the accident was discovered. The car was engulfed in flames when rescuers arrived. Two bodies were pulled from the wreck—burned beyond recognition.

Only after the license plate was identified did officials contact the family at La Colombaia. There had been a third passenger, they were told. The wreckage was searched again.

Tuomas was found—alive.

He spent eight days in a coma at a hospital in Florence before doctors allowed his father, Olli Arkko, to fly him by air ambulance to Helsinki. Tuomas remembered nothing—not the accident, not the hospital, not the weeks that followed.

The news of Angela and Carlo's deaths stunned the family. Some feared that Sofia, Carlo's widow, would lose her mind. Others worried Nonna Olivia would suffer a heart attack from grief.

But neither woman broke.

Angela and Carlo were cremated together, their ashes placed side by side in the Costa family grave.

Olli did not attend the funeral. Tuomas was still in critical condition, and Olli refused to leave his son's side. He also carried a quiet guilt. He had taken Angela—Pietro Costa's only daughter—away to Finland. And it was during that she had died.

After the memorial service, Sofia continued running Ristorante La Colombaia, with the help of Olivia and the village women. Life resumed its rhythm, though quieter now.

Olivia made her way down to the valley several times a week, walking slowly to the family grave. Dressed in black, she would sit on the mossy stone bench like a statue. So still, the cemetery sparrows sometimes dared to perch on her shawl.

Only her whisper could be heard.

"Holy Mother of God... thank you for protecting my children from the revenge of the lava people."

11

When Tuomas finally woke from his coma, he was disoriented, pale, and weak. His body ached, and time felt slippery—like something half-remembered from a dream.

The first thing he asked was, "Why hasn't Mom come to see me?"

Olli Arkko froze. For days, he had dreaded this moment. He'd rehearsed explanations, softened truths, and imagined a hundred ways to delay the question. But now, with his son staring at him—confused, hopeful—there was nowhere left to hide.

He sat down gently on the edge of the hospital bed.

"I didn't want to tell you until you were stronger," he said, voice thick. "But you deserve the truth."

Tuomas's eyes widened. "What happened?"

"She didn't survive the accident."

There was a long silence.

Olli opened his arms, and Tuomas fell into them, sobbing against his chest. The boy's body was still fragile, but the grief in him surged with unexpected force.

They held each other like that for a long time—father and son, tethered now by loss.

"I only have you now," Olli whispered. "But we'll make it. Somehow, we'll get through this."

Tuomas sniffled, wiping his face on the edge of the blanket. "What about Chiara and Nonna? What did they say when they heard about Uncle Carlo?"

"La Colombaia is... carrying on," Olli said. "I've called a few times, but you know my Italian isn't great. Nonna always asks for you. She'd love to hear your voice."

Tuomas looked down at his hands, his brow furrowed. "Before we left... Nonna gave me her necklace. She said Saint Christopher would protect me."

Olli hesitated. "The gold chain...?"

He remembered it arriving in a small plastic bag with Tuomas's personal effects—scuffed shoes, a torn T-shirt, and that strange chain with a dark stone. He hadn't thought much of it at the time. Just another piece of jewelry from Angela's collection, maybe a gift she'd picked up for Tuomas during their vacation.

"I put it in your mom's jewelry box," he added. "I didn't realize it came from Olivia."

Tuomas reached up to his chest instinctively, surprised not to feel the weight of the pendant. He frowned.

"I want it back," he said softly.

Olli nodded. "Of course. I'll bring it to you."

And as he stood and crossed the room, something in Tuomas's gaze lingered—like an echo of heat from a fire long since burned out. A flicker of memory? A whisper from somewhere deeper?

Whatever it was, the pendant was calling.

12

People had always admired three things about Tuomas. First: his father's car. Olli Arkko had received the elegant black Alfa Romeo as a reward for saving the life of an Arab prince during his years as a private pilot in the Emirates—long before Tuomas was born. Though Olli now flew for a commercial airline, he had kept the car. Tuomas loved the moment the engine roared to life. It felt like sitting on the back of a wild animal—its muscles coiled, ready to leap.

Second: his father himself. At six-foot-three, Olli Arkko was already an imposing figure. But in his crisp captain's uniform, stepping out of the black Alfa, he drew every eye.

And third—Tuomas. More precisely, his fiery red hair. Once, people stared in admiration.

But not today.

Today, the looks were different. Not wonder.

As Tuomas struggled out of the car with his crutches, their stares seemed to say: Poor child. And worse: Poor man, having to carry a broken boy like that.

"We're here," his father said quietly, steering the car off the main road into a narrow, shady lane lined with oaks.

Tuomas braced himself for more stares, more pity. But when they pulled up in front of the old manor house, there was no one waiting. No welcoming committee.

Tuomas glared out the window.

Damn old red house.

Damn weathered outbuilding.

Damn crumbling windmill in the field.

This was the last place his father should have brought him.

But Tuomas was wrong to think no one had noticed their arrival.

High on the wing of the gray windmill sat a strange creature dressed in black leather, swinging its feet. With eyes glowing like red embers, it watched the sleek black car roll to a stop.

Then the creature slid down from the wing, tugged at a ring in its nose, changed shape, and melted into the tall grass.

Inside the car, Olli leaned back and massaged his temples. That migraine again. He sighed and turned to his son.

"This is it. The Arkko farm. My parents' house."

"I don't want to stay here."

"This is your place now."

"I want to live with you. In Helsinki. In your house."

"That's not going to happen." Olli's voice was flat. "Enough talk. You're a big boy now. You have to be strong. None of this is easy for me either."

He got out of the car.

Suddenly, the patio door flew open, and a plump woman with gray hair and a flour-covered white baker's cap came waddling out, waving both hands and shouting something Tuomas couldn't understand.

She bustled down the stairs, laughing and chattering in a warm, chaotic tumble. Olli greeted her with a hug.

"Alma!"

"Careful, Olli! I'm covered in flour!" she scolded, beaming.

"We didn't expect you so soon."

"With a good car, it's faster."

"We missed you both so much."

"Really?"

A second figure appeared at the top of the stairs—a tall woman in an elegant gray dress. She watched the scene silently, arms folded, brow furrowed.

"Alma," she said curtly, "please continue with your work."

"In a moment. But isn't it nice Olli came home with the boy?" Alma replied, smiling.

"Hello, Mama," Olli said.

The woman didn't step down to greet him. She stood still.

"So here we are," he said.

"So it seems," she replied coldly.

"Can your son get out by himself," she asked, "or is he waiting for an invitation?"

Olli opened the back door. He pulled out the crutches, leaned them against the car, unbuckled Tuomas, and carefully lifted him out.

"This is Tuomas. Say hello to your grandmother."

"I'm not a grandmother. And I'm certainly not a grandma," the woman said sharply. "You can call me Irma. Like everyone else."

Her voice was rough as bark, and it sent a chill through Tuomas. So this was his Finnish grandmother.

In Italy, the moment they'd arrived at La Colombaia, relatives had swarmed the car. Nonna Olivia had squeezed and kissed him until his mother had to pull her off, laughing. Everyone had talked at once. There had been warmth.

This? This was ice.

Tuomas looked at the woman on the steps. He could see where his father got his looks—tall, blond, upright, almost noble. Regal and remote.

As if reading his thoughts, Irma sniffed. "The boy looks like his mother. No trace of the Arkko family."

"Mother, please," Olli said.

"Can he even speak?" Irma asked, her eyes narrowing at Tuomas, who stood braced on his crutches.

"Don't be ridiculous," Olli snapped. "Of course he can talk. He speaks Finnish, Italian, and a little English. His legs are healing. He'll be walking again soon."

"Good. Alma, since you're here, take Mr. Tuomas to his room," Irma said briskly, turning back toward the house. "And get rid of that wretched cat!"

A sleek black cat had appeared on the steps, licking its paw in lazy defiance.

Alma rolled her eyes and shrugged at Olli.

She turned to Tuomas. "Can you manage, or should I help?"

"I can manage," Tuomas said, more sharply than he intended.

"Don't worry. She warms up—eventually."

As Olli began unloading the suitcase, Tuomas and Alma started up the steps toward the manor house.

"Need help with the stairs?" Alma asked.

"No, thank you. I've got it."

Tuomas gritted his teeth and dragged himself upward. The black cat followed, slinking along the railing, tail twitching.

Was it… watching him?

No. Laughing.

He stared at the animal. Its eyes glinted—not green or yellow, but red. Tuomas blinked.

Was that a metal ring in its nose?

Surely not. Nose rings were for bulls in Spanish arenas… not cats.

And yet.

13

The boy followed Alma through the wide hall and down a long corridor. The walls were lined with dark portraits in heavy gilt frames. Antique wicker chairs sat in the window recesses, and bright red flowers bloomed defiantly on the windowsills, their petals like small flames against the gloom.

Alma waddled ahead, glancing over her shoulder several times to make sure Tuomas wasn't lagging behind.

"You can call me Alma, like your father does," she said over her shoulder. "And I'm not calling you Mr. Tuomas—kids today are spoiled enough already. And her—not wanting to be called a grandmother! For heaven's sake, you're her only grandchild. She should be happy you're here." Alma snorted in disapproval.

They reached the end of the hall, where Alma opened a door and gestured inside.

"By the way, this was your father's room."

Tuomas stepped in and looked around. The room was sparsely furnished: brown cupboards, a tall bookcase, a large, old-fashioned desk, a few stiff chairs, a creaky rocking chair, and a narrow bed covered with a colorful wool blanket. A red-striped rag rug lay at the foot of the bed, adding a splash of life to the otherwise drab space.

Alma looked at the rug for a moment, then bent down, rolled it up, and carried it into the hallway.

"So you won't trip on your crutches," she explained matter-of-factly.

Then she drew back the gray curtains, releasing a soft cloud of dust into the sunlight. Beyond the window stretched an old garden filled with gnarled apple trees that bled into farmland. In the distance stood a weathered windmill, its arms still against the sky.

Tuomas made his way to the bed and eased himself onto it.

"Can't you take a step without the crutches?" Alma asked, concern flickering in her voice.

"I don't dare," Tuomas admitted. "I'm afraid I'll fall. If the bones break again, I might never walk properly."

"Don't worry, we'll find a solution," she said. "And if we don't… well, we'll ask Jaska."

"Who's Jaska? A doctor?"

"Jaska… oh, forget Jaska," Alma said quickly. "If your father hasn't told you about him, it's probably better that way. And don't mention him around your grandmother."

Tuomas was about to press the matter when something on the wall caught his attention. He pointed to a yellowed photograph in a carved wooden frame.

"Is that Dad?"

Alma nodded.

"And that's Grandma—I mean Irma. But who's the girl?"

Alma sighed. Her eyes lingered on the photo for a long moment before she answered.

"That's Seijaliisa. Your father's sister. Your aunt."

"My aunt?" Tuomas frowned. "She never visited us."

"No. She didn't. Seijaliisa died shortly after that picture was taken. She was only twenty. It was a terrible time for your grandmother—and for all of us. Best not to talk about it."

That makes three things I'm not allowed to talk about, Tuomas thought. Jaska. Seijaliisa. What next? Maybe I need to keep a list.

He glanced at Alma. "Was it a car accident?" he asked carefully, watching for any sign of irritation.

"No, not at all," Alma said, her voice softer now. "She'd had an appendectomy. Everything seemed fine afterward. But no one knew she was highly allergic to wasp stings. It was summer, and the window in her room had been left open during the day. Maybe a wasp crawled into her bedding and stung her in her sleep."

Tuomas's mouth dropped slightly. "That's awful."

"Your grandmother had insisted on a private room for her," Alma went on. "Said she needed peace and quiet to recover. Maybe if she'd had a roommate, someone might've gotten help in time. Irma doesn't talk about it, but I think it still haunts her."

They sat in silence for a moment.

Tuomas's eyes went back to the photo. "And what about Grandpa? I think that's him, right?"

"Yes," Alma said. "It hit him hard too. But he still had your father. Though Olli didn't want to stay here long—he joined the army, became a pilot, and flew far away. After that, it was just the three of us trying to keep things going."

Tuomas hesitated. "And then the tsunami came? Dad told me."

Alma nodded slowly. "Yes. He was traveling alone. Your grandmother had stayed home. Lucky, I suppose."

Tuomas made a mental note: Topic number four—off-limits with Irma: the tsunami.

"Don't bring it up with her," Alma said, echoing his thoughts. "It's… difficult."

Tuomas exhaled. Four forbidden topics. This place is like a museum with locked exhibits. He felt like a ghost among ghosts.

14

In the hallway, the sound of suitcases being dragged across the uneven floorboards echoed like reluctant footsteps. Tuomas looked up as his father appeared in the doorway.

"Well," Olli said, surveying the room. "Now you've seen it. Not much to look at."

He glanced at the bare furnishings, then added, "Alma, could you sew some brighter curtains? We could hang some posters too—maybe the Statue of Liberty, when I fly to New York tomorrow."

"Tomorrow?" Tuomas asked, stunned. "You're not staying overnight?"

"Unfortunately, I have to head back to Helsinki today. It's better to sleep in your own bed before a long flight. And departure's early in the morning."

Tuomas stared at him, frozen. He's leaving me. Today.

The thought pressed like ice against his chest. His father was really going to leave him here—with the cold-eyed grandmother and the staring portraits of dead relatives. He blinked hard, willing back the tears.

Don't let him see. Don't cry. Not in front of him. Men don't cry. At least not Arkko men.

"I'll unpack after dinner and put your things in the closet," Alma offered gently. Even she didn't sound happy about Olli's quick departure.

Olli stepped forward and ran his hand through Tuomas's unruly red hair. "I still need to talk to your grandmother about your school and a few other things. Get some rest—it's been a long trip. Alma will come get you when dinner's ready."

From the hallway, a dull voice rose—the hum of a television. Olli tilted his head.

Has she gone deaf now? he wondered. I'll have to remind Tuomas to speak up if he wants her to hear a word he says.

He knocked once on the library door. No answer.

He opened it.

His mother, Irma, sat stiffly in the only soft chair in the room. The others were stiff-backed and upholstered in cracked leather, like something out of an English manor.

A stack of books sat untouched on the side table. Olli doubted she had opened one in years. Books were for Seijaliisa. Mother had once banned her daughter from borrowing from the town library—"too many fingerprints from people with bad habits." She had insisted on new, untouched editions, shipped in by catalog, each carefully selected to mold Seijaliisa into the perfect wife for a perfect future son-in-law.

Rich. Famous. Powerful.

Instead, Seijaliisa had died of a wasp sting, alone in a hospital bed.

Irma lowered the volume on the television but didn't look at him.

Olli sat across from her. A long silence followed.

Then she spoke.

"How could you do this to me, Olavi?"

He didn't answer.

"First you marry a woman who couldn't cope with life in this house—who couldn't even cope with Finland. And then in that job—"

"Mother." Olli's voice was low but firm. "I fly too. And being a flight attendant is just as respectable."

She sniffed. "Fine. But then you dump a boy I don't even know in my lap. One who needs to be looked after like a baby. At my age. What's the point?"

"You didn't want to know him," Olli said coldly. "After that one visit, you stopped calling. Angela and Tuomas never heard from you again. He's not a baby. He'll walk on his own soon enough. The doctors are confident."

Irma crossed her arms.

"You should've left him in Italy. Your wife has family there—he was always with them anyway."

"It's easier for me to see him here," Olli said. "I'm in Helsinki between flights. He's already enrolled in school there, and I want him to finish his education in Finland. The schools are better."

"You could put him in boarding school," she said bluntly. "You can afford it."

"He's not ready for boarding school. And I wouldn't want that for him anyway. This is my childhood home. Tuomas belongs here. And whether you like it or not—you're his grandmother."

"I hate that word," she said sharply. "Makes me sound ready for a nursing home."

"At least Alma is still here," Olli muttered.

"Alma has enough to do."

"I could hire someone to help."

"I don't want any more strangers in the house. If Alma agrees to care for the boy, fine. But if he causes trouble, he's out."

After Alma and his father had left the room, Tuomas climbed into bed. He was more exhausted from the trip than he'd let on. Carefully, he placed his elbow crutches at the foot of the bed, within easy reach.

Despite the mild early summer air, he pulled the dark brown blanket up to his chin. The weight of it felt comforting, like a shield against everything unfamiliar.

Now that his father could no longer see him, the tears came. They welled quietly in his eyes, spilling down his cheeks before he could stop them.

Daddy is going back to Helsinki today.

Tuomas had imagined this would be different. He thought his father would stay at the family house for at least a few days—show him the secret corners of his childhood, hidden places in the attic or garden, maybe an old hideout near the windmill. Surely even a place like this held some kind of magic?

He had hoped his father would help him find his bearings in this creaking, unfamiliar house. Help him figure out how to navigate everything—on crutches.

He had also hoped to get to know his grandmother better—though he was already careful not to call her that. Irma. Cold, distant Irma. But maybe, just maybe, there was something kind buried under all that frost.

And Alma—he already liked her. He'd taken to calling her Alma Mater in his head. He'd read that mater meant "mother" in Latin, and somehow the name fit. Maybe Alma had even been more of a mother to his father than Irma had ever been.

Now, she would be the one caring for him too.

He looked out the window. No other houses. No kids. No sign of neighbors or friendly strangers. Just the big, brooding manor, the overgrown garden, and fields stretching endlessly into the distance.

The only thing that had greeted him was that strange black cat on the stairs.

How could his father leave him here?

Only two days ago, he had been discharged from the rehab clinic in Helsinki. Two days at home, and now—this.

The ache in his chest spread like a quiet weight.

Tuomas thought about it all—his mother, the accident, this strange house—and let sleep slowly take him.

After leaving his mother in the library, Olli headed to the kitchen.

Alma was rinsing crisp heads of lettuce from the garden under the tap. The scent of damp soil and fresh greens filled the room.

"Have you seen Jaska?" Olli asked quietly.

Alma didn't look up. "Not for a long time," she said. "Maybe he's changed so much I wouldn't recognize him anymore. Maybe he's angry with me. With all of us."

She set the lettuce aside and wiped her hands on her apron.

"He was already strange when you left," she continued. "Once, he looked like some kind of punk—with rings in his ears and a chain in his nose. Then he turned up pretending to be Prince William, just because he knew I had a soft spot for that boy."

Olli laughed. "In my day, he pretended to be Elvis."

"Because you loved Elvis," Alma said, smiling. "A few years ago, he said his name was Tsakko—not Jaska anymore—and he moved around like a spring-loaded puppet. Told me it was something called a moonwalk. He must have seen it on Irma's TV when he was spying."

"Tsakko?" Olli raised an eyebrow, then chuckled. "You mean Jacko. Michael Jackson."

Alma nodded. "Yes, that's it."

"Tuomas liked Michael Jackson too," Olli said, his voice dipping. "Tried to dance like him. Before the accident."

They both fell silent for a moment.

"Do you think he'll recover?" Alma asked gently.

"The doctors are hopeful. The last surgery went well. Physically, he's healing." Olli looked down, as if the truth might be hiding somewhere on Alma's tiled floor. "But he's lost his courage. Especially after Angela died. I try to be there for him, but I'm always away with work. He was well cared for at the clinic, but…"

Alma shook her head sadly. "Poor boy. No mother. A father who's barely around. And a grandmother as cold as a freezer."

"Don't exaggerate," Olli said, though without much conviction. "Mom is starting to warm up to him. He's a good kid."

"How did you manage to warm up?" Alma asked.

"The work helped. It kept my head busy. No time to think. But whenever I came back to Helsinki and sat by Tuomas' hospital bed... I saw Angela in his face. Every time. And that made it harder."

Olli's voice caught. "He felt that, I think. My distance. He's been so lonely. He left behind the only new friends he'd made at the clinic. Now it's just us."

"Us?" Alma gave him a pointed look.

"You, I mean. You're the one who's here," Olli said softly. "Maybe you can help. Maybe even Jaska."

Alma sighed and leaned against the counter.

"Jaska," she murmured. "The last time I saw him clearly was after the storm. When the windmill's wings broke."

Olli looked up.

"The villagers came to fix it on their own," she said, half to herself. "No one asked them to. I was sweeping up the broken wood, and Jaska appeared—just like that. Greeted me like nothing had happened. But he was already fading. Almost transparent. Like the idea of him was slipping away."

She looked over at Olli. "Maybe one day he'll vanish for good. When I'm gone. When there's no one left to believe in him."

15

Tuomas heard the door open. Alma entered, carrying a tray that filled the room with the warm, comforting aroma of food.

"You're already awake," she said cheerfully. "I made lasagna—I thought you might like something Mediterranean."

Tuomas gave a small nod as he pushed himself up on his elbows.

"Don't you want to change into something more comfortable?" Alma asked as she set the tray down. "And I haven't even asked—can you get to the bathroom by yourself? It's right down the hall."

Tuomas flushed. Alma clearly meant well, but her concern made him squirm.

"I can manage," he said quickly. "And my clothes are fine."

On the way to the dining room, Tuomas passed the old piano in the entrance hall. Its lid was thick with dust, but curiosity got the better of him. He hobbled over, lifted the lid, and pressed a few quiet keys.

Alma screamed from behind him. "Don't touch that! You mustn't play it!"

Startled, Tuomas turned.

"That was Seijaliisa's piano," she said in a hushed voice. "Only she ever played it. I hope Irma didn't hear…"

Another thing to add to the list of forbidden topics, Tuomas thought, amused despite himself. No Jaska. No Seijaliisa. No piano.

Alma opened the door to the dining room. It didn't seem as though Irma had heard, but the air in the room was heavy, like the moments before a thunderstorm.

The long wooden table was set as if for a dinner party — polished glasses, neatly folded napkins, and a vase of early summer flowers at the center. Tuomas was surprised. The table was set for three.

Alma helped him into his chair before hurrying back to the kitchen. The smell of fresh bread rose from a basket near his plate. For a brief moment, Tuomas was back in Nonna Olivia's warm kitchen in Tuscany.

But now, Irma and Olli sat stiffly at opposite ends of the table, and Tuomas was stuck between them like a question nobody wanted to answer.

The only sound was the slow, measured ticking of the tall grandfather clock against the far wall.

"Olavi, stop rocking in your chair," Irma snapped. "You've already broken one of the legs."

Olli immediately stopped, but soon began drumming his fingers on the edge of the table.

"You're making me nervous," she said sharply.

At that moment, the grandfather clock struck twice, breaking the silence — and the tension.

Alma returned, pushing a trolley into the room. On it was a steaming casserole dish of lasagna, a large bowl of salad, and a glass jar of homemade dressing. She stopped beside Irma and began to serve.

Irma eyed the food warily. "What have you made now?"

"I thought I'd try a light oven dish," Alma said. "Lasagna. I think Tuomas will like it."

"We're not starting new traditions now," Irma muttered. "We're Finnish. We eat Finnish food."

"They eat lasagna in Finland too," Olli said mildly.

"And salad," Alma added, pouring dressing onto the leaves. "I even made the dressing myself. Because last time…"

She caught herself, suddenly quiet.

Ten years ago, there had been no dressing at the table—just neat bowls of dry cucumber and tomato slices. Tuomas's mother, visiting for the first and only time, had whispered to Olli in English that the salad tasted like hay meant for cattle. "In Italy," she had said, "even the simplest salad has olive oil and vinegar." Olli had tried to soften the comment in translation, but Irma's answer had been cold and direct.

"Every nation has its customs. Either you adapt, or you leave."

Alma remembered it well. She didn't need to be told twice.

She quietly served the rest of the food—white wine for Irma, water for Olli and Tuomas. Then, wordlessly, she took the flower vase from the table and left the room, closing the door behind her.

Irma noticed Tuomas's surprised glance.

"Alma eats in the kitchen," she said. "In proper households, servants dine separately."

Tuomas met his father's eyes across the table. Olli raised an eyebrow—a silent message: Don't argue.

The lasagna was a revelation. After months of hospital food—bland and under-seasoned—it was rich and satisfying. Tuomas cleaned his plate, to Alma's quiet delight when she peeked back in later.

After the meal, Olli leaned back and turned to his son.

"As I said, I have to return to Helsinki tonight. But I'll be back for Midsummer. We'll spend a few days together then."

Then he looked to Irma.

"Tuomas needs to continue his physical therapy. Twice a week in the city. Maybe Alma can go with him. Or you could arrange a taxi. The insurance covers it. If the therapist recommends anything else—equipment, exercises— I'll pay for it."

"Alma can manage it," Irma said. "I have other things to do."

"If all goes well, he can start school after summer. If not…"

"I don't want to go to boarding school!" Tuomas blurted.

"I wasn't suggesting that," Olli said. "I was thinking of a governess."

"A governess?" Irma scoffed. "What century are you living in?"

"If I recall, you trained as a teacher in Arvola before marrying my father," Olli said calmly.

"That was more than forty years ago. Teaching is different now. And I'm not about to become your son's teacher."

Olli didn't reply. He stood and began to gather the dishes, a quiet sign that the conversation was over.

16

After lunch, Tuomas's father offered to show him the house. Tuomas followed, leaning on his crutches. They started in the kitchen, where they thanked Alma again for the delicious meal.

Alma's kitchen was a mix of old and new. A modern electric stove stood beside a giant, well-worn oven. Shelves lined the walls, filled with dishes, and heavy pots hung from hooks in the ceiling.

"Remind me to give Tuomas his medicine before I leave," Olli said.

There were so many rooms on the ground floor that Tuomas quickly lost track of where his own was. Every hallway seemed to lead to another wing, another set of closed doors.

A wide spiral staircase rose from the entrance hall.

"Just empty rooms up there now," Olli said. "There used to be more people living here. Cooks, maids, servants… Alma probably still lives upstairs."

He turned to his son. "Now I'm going to show you something special. Still got the strength to continue?"

Tuomas was already tired, but his father's mysterious smile stirred his curiosity. He nodded.

They walked down a second corridor, away from the main hall. At the end stood a massive double door. Olli pushed it open and led Tuomas inside.

Tuomas's eyes widened.

He hadn't expected this.

The room was vast. The walls were built from thick, dark beams, and the floorboards were nearly as wide as the benches that lined the sides. Long wooden tables stretched the length of the hall. Faded carpets hung from the walls, their colors muted by time. Sunlight filtered in through high, narrow windows, casting golden stripes across the floor.

"This is where the Kestikievari's customers used to be entertained," Olli said.

Tuomas blinked. "What's a Kestikievari?"

"It was like an inn. Back before cars, people traveled by boat or carriage. Steamboats would dock at the shore below the farm, and passengers would come up here to wait for their next ride—or spend the night. This place was always full of travelers."

He gestured around the room.

"That's why there are so many guest rooms in the house. But when cars came and roads got better, no one needed the steamboats anymore. Business died. By the time your grandfather was in charge, this was just a regular farm."

Tuomas looked around again, imagining strangers eating, talking, warming themselves by the fire. "Was Grandpa a farmer?"

"Not really," Olli said. "He was more interested in horse racing and traveling. He rented the fields out, sold the livestock, let the staff go. Eventually, it was just us."

Tuomas hesitated, then asked, "Are there no animals now?"

He had hoped there might be a watchdog like Bruno at La Colombaia—or maybe even a pony he could pet.

"Just the cat," Olli said with a shrug. "Maybe. I'm not even sure if it belongs to us. Ask Alma."

Tuomas nodded. He had a feeling Alma knew everything about the house.

Next to the door stood a huge brick oven built into the wall. A narrow flight of stairs led upward.

"After a long journey, travelers would warm themselves here," Olli explained. "If someone fell into an icy lake, they'd be brought in and laid by the fire. If they didn't ask for a beer within half an hour, they'd be taken to the granary—on the corpse board."

Tuomas's eyes went wide. "They put dead people on the stove?"

Before Olli could answer, Alma's voice rang out.

"What nonsense are you filling the boy's head with now?" she scolded, stepping through a side door.

"Is the house haunted?" Tuomas asked her. "It's old enough."

Alma snorted. "I wish we had ghosts! Would make things more lively. Maybe a few house elves, but that's it."

She turned to Olli. "Let the boy rest. He's had a long day."

Tuomas was secretly amused. Both Irma and Alma treated Olli like a schoolboy who still needed scolding. It made him feel just a little better.

That evening, Tuomas didn't say goodbye when his father left. He pretended to be asleep when Olli came into the room. His father placed something on the desk—Tuomas didn't move. He heard the soft click of the door closing, then the crunch of gravel under tires as the car rolled away down the long drive.

Later, Tuomas sat up and looked around. On his desk were a tablet and a small printer—his father had brought them earlier.

"We can Skype," Olli had promised. "No matter where I am."

Tuomas already knew how to track his father's flights. He'd watch the little digital plane crawl from America across the Atlantic or over the Pacific to Tokyo or Singapore. He could also video call his family in Italy. Chiara already had a tablet too.

Still, none of that helped with the silence.

Now, in the dim quiet of the manor house, with only two old women living under its sagging roof—one of whom clearly didn't want him there—Tuomas felt lonelier than ever.

There was a soft knock at the door.

Alma stepped inside, carrying a tray with cheese sandwiches, a glass of juice, a yogurt, and a shiny red apple.

"I'm bringing your food to your room today so you can have a little peace and quiet," she said, setting the tray on the desk. "I've already put your things in the closet. Call me on my cell if you need anything—day or night. Here's my number—put it in your phone. I'll be there in no time."

At least Alma had a cell phone. No one else in the house did, and certainly not a computer. Tuomas remembered how his father had asked if there was Wi-Fi. Alma had waved it off with a laugh. "What would we do with that? Who would even use it?"

No computer. Not even interested. Tuomas could hardly believe it. He thought people like that only existed in fairy tales or forest cabins.

"Well," Alma had said, patting the doorframe before she left. "We'll see how tomorrow goes."

That night, Tuomas woke with a start, gasping.

His own scream had pulled him out of sleep. He'd been lying twisted in the strange bed, his hip throbbing, his skin drenched in sweat. The blanket had slid halfway off the bed.

But that wasn't what had woken him.

Something was wrong.

He didn't dare move or open his eyes. Still, he knew—with every hair on his neck standing up—that he wasn't alone.

It wasn't Alma. Alma smelled like mint and chives and basil—like pasta sauce. This... whatever it was... had no scent at all. No breath. Just a presence. Heavy. Still. Watching.

It was over by the rocking chair.

Very slowly, Tuomas pushed the blanket down from his face and opened one eye.

The room was dimly lit by the pale spring moon filtering through the curtains. Everything looked quiet.

Then the rocking chair moved.

Just once—back and forth.

Ghosts.

Tuomas yanked the blanket back over his head and squeezed his eyes shut. He stayed like that, holding his breath, until his body finally relaxed and sleep took him again.

He awoke when someone tugged the blanket from his face.

His heart jumped—but it was only Alma, smiling down at him, the curtains already flung open behind her.

"You were suffocating under there, poor child. Were you cold?" she asked, brushing a hand across his forehead. "How did you sleep? First night in a new bed is never easy."

Tuomas sat up slowly. "Were you... in here last night?"

Alma gave him a curious look. "How could I be? No."

"Oh. I just... I thought maybe I dreamed someone was here."

She raised an eyebrow, then smiled again, unfazed. "Time for breakfast. Your grandmother has already eaten. We let you sleep in this morning. Normally, meals are in the dining room—you are, after all, the young master of the Arkko estate."

Young master. Tuomas nearly laughed. He never imagined he'd be part of a place like this—an old house filled with ancestral paintings and dusty secrets. Yet here he was. His father's only heir, just as his father had once been.

Alma handed him a glass of water and a small bottle of pills.

"Take your medicine—it'll help build you up. And we'll take care of the rest with good food and fresh air. Tomorrow, we head into the city for your physical therapy. Today, we'll take a little tour of the village. We'll see the school, stop by the market, maybe even the beach. If the water's warm enough, I'll take you swimming. You might meet some local kids."

Tuomas perked up. "Swimming?"

"Of course! You'll find it easier to move in the water—the water will carry you." She smiled. "Can you swim already?"

Alma kept talking, rattling off plans as if she hadn't had anyone to talk to for years. Maybe she hadn't. Irma certainly wasn't the chatty type.

"Can you really drive?" Tuomas asked, still half in disbelief.

Alma grinned. "Had to learn. Your grandmother doesn't like errands. She's more interested in city fashion shops and concerts. She's got her own car for that sort of thing."

After breakfast, Alma rolled her little red Beetle out of the garage and pulled it up to the front door. Tuomas watched in astonishment as she managed to squeeze her round frame behind the wheel with practiced ease. She buckled him in first, humming to herself, then got in and started the engine.

Tuomas had to admit—it felt good to get out of the house.

Even if he wasn't sure whether something had been in his room the night before.

17

Their first stop was the village school in Arvola. To Tuomas's relief, it wasn't an old, crumbling wooden hut like he'd feared. The building was large and modern, with wide hallways and even an elevator from the assembly hall to the upper floors.

Alma had already arranged everything with the headmistress. She led Tuomas confidently through the quiet corridors. Fortunately, there was no recess at that hour—no students around to stare or whisper. For now, he was spared the curious looks he dreaded.

What would they have thought anyway? he wondered bitterly. Who's that scarecrow with elbow crutches? Is coming to our school? Hope not in our class!

The headmaster greeted them outside the office. He wasn't what Tuomas had expected. Tall, broad-shouldered, and wearing a red-striped T-shirt that clung to his muscles, he looked more like a bodybuilder than a teacher.

He shook Tuomas's hand firmly. "So, you're in fourth grade," he said, guiding them into a small office. Papers were spread out across the desk.

"Let's see how well you'll be able to keep up," the principal said. "After such a serious accident, it wouldn't be surprising if your memory, or more, had been affected."

"My brain is fine! It's been checked—several times!" Tuomas blurted out, his voice sharper than intended.

Alma nudged him in the ribs. One didn't raise their voice to a principal—not in Finland, anyway.

The man raised his hands in a calming gesture. "That's good to hear. We also have a school assistant who can help if there are any challenges. Would you like to meet your future class before the summer break?"

"That would be perfect," Alma answered before Tuomas had a chance to say no.

"Class 3A is in English right now. You're welcome to join them."

"3A?" Tuomas frowned. "They're younger than me! I was in third grade last year. I should've started fourth in the fall—back in Helsinki!"

The principal nodded, unfazed. "Yes, but you missed a whole school year. That puts you behind. Still, if you make good progress, we can move you up midyear. There are other students your age in 3A—migrant kids, students who need extra support… even a blind girl."

Exactly what Tuomas had feared.

The principal knocked on the classroom door, and when it opened, all conversation inside ceased. Eyes turned toward the doorway.

A student whispered, "It's the cripple."

The headmaster cleared his throat. "A new student will be joining your class after summer break. This is Tuomas Arkko. I hope you'll welcome him and be good friends."

He turned to the teacher. "Can take him with her whenever you think it's best. Official classes won't start until after the holidays."

He flashed a charming smile and left the room.

The teacher, a short, round woman with kind eyes, blinked in surprise, then smiled at Tuomas. "I'm your homeroom teacher—Paula Puntanen. But everyone calls me Paula. You can sit next to Miranda. That chair's free. Mrs. Lampinen, feel free to sit in the back if you'd like to follow along."

Tuomas hobbled forward on his crutches and sat down beside the girl named Miranda. She gave him a quick "Hello" and returned to her book.

Tuomas noticed something strange—her eyes were just as blue as his. But there was something else. She held her face very close to the pages and ran her fingers across the paper as she read.

Tuomas leaned over. Her book wasn't made of normal print—it was full of raised dots. Braille.

Miranda was blind.

And yet, none of the other students reacted to how she read. No one stared or whispered. To them, it was clearly normal.

Tuomas watched in fascination. He'd heard of Braille, but had never seen someone actually read with their fingertips. It was like magic.

"Tuomas, would you like to read the next sentence?" Paula asked. "Did you study English at your last school?"

"Mirko, let Tuomas borrow your book for a moment."

A boy with greasy neck-length hair scowled at Tuomas, but slid the book across the desk and jabbed his finger at the correct line.

Tuomas began slowly, hesitantly. But the words came back to him, and soon he was reading more confidently—by the end of the page, he was reading aloud with ease.

Paula's face lit up. "Well, I think we've found a natural. Where did you learn to speak English so well?"

Tuomas blushed. He hadn't meant to stand out—not in front of strangers. The class stared at him as if he were an alien who had just landed from space.

"I…"

Alma spoke from the back of the room. "Tuomas has traveled a lot. His father is an airline captain."

Great. That was the last thing Tuomas needed. Now the village kids would think he was some rich outsider with a fancy life. He could already imagine the teasing.

The recess bell rang. Alma came to help him up.

"I think that's enough for today," she said to Paula. "We've got a few more things to do."

"Welcome back after the holidays," Paula said, giving Tuomas an encouraging smile. She seemed kind. Maybe school here wouldn't be so bad.

The class still stared, silent and curious.

All except Miranda.

She sat calmly, tracing her fingers along the Braille page. Tuomas felt a sudden wave of relief. She wouldn't see his awkward gait. She wouldn't judge his crutches. And she'd never say anything about his red hair.

18

After Tuomas' first physical therapy session in the city, he was completely worn out. The therapist had told him it would be a long road—building strength in his legs would take time, and patience was the key. Under no circumstances should he try to walk without crutches or other aids, at least not until school started.

Grumbling, Tuomas returned home with Alma, but he didn't want to go inside. Frustrated, he dropped onto the front steps of the porch. The early summer air was warm and filled with the scent of pine and lilac, birds chirped in the trees, and sunlight dappled the yard. But Tuomas felt none of it. He cursed his misery.

Then something shifted inside him—some quiet fire stirred, the stubbornness that Finns call sisu.

I don't need these crutches. I can walk. I will walk.

Gritting his teeth, Tuomas pushed himself up with the crutches, tossed them aside with sudden defiance, and took a step across the sandy yard. He made it one step. Then another.

But by the third, his legs buckled.

He would've collapsed face-first if someone hadn't grabbed him from behind—strong hands hooked under his arms and pulled him upright.

A rough voice hissed in his ear, "Pride comes before a fall... but the brave eat the rat."

And then the grip released.

Tuomas stumbled, swaying, but didn't fall. He spun around to see who had caught him.

No one was there.

Suddenly, the crutches he'd thrown beside the steps began to move. All by themselves. They skidded across the yard as if tugged by invisible hands and came to a gentle stop right at his side—upright, perfectly placed in front of him. His hands trembled as he grabbed them.

This place is really haunted.

Tuomas turned and scrambled back to the porch. Just as he reached the steps, the front door creaked open and Alma stepped out, smiling as if nothing were out of the ordinary.

Still shaking, Tuomas clung to the railing.

"So," Alma said with a twinkle in her eye, "you've met Jaska."

Tuomas gaped at her. "What?"

"I saw it from the kitchen window. I was ready to run out if you fell," Alma admitted, wiping her hands on her apron. "But you didn't fall, did you?"

"There was no one there."

"Well, Jaska was there. You just didn't see him."

Tuomas looked around nervously. "Who… what is Jaska?"

"Hard to explain," Alma said, sitting beside him on the step. "He's not a ghost, not really. More like a spirit. A house spirit, maybe. He's been here as long as anyone can remember."

"A ghost spirit?" Tuomas asked, unsure whether to laugh or cry.

"Not a ghost," Alma said. "Not scary. Shy, mostly. He doesn't always show himself. It takes time for him to trust someone."

"He talked to me," Tuomas whispered. "Well—he said something. Weird."

"Typical Jaska. He hasn't spoken to people in years. His sayings are a bit scrambled. You have to get used to it."

"Is he always invisible?"

"Not always. He used to show himself to me. And to your father when he was young."

"Dad knows about Jaska?" Tuomas asked, surprised and a little relieved.

"Of course. Your father hopes you and Jaska will become friends. Because if no one believes in him anymore, he'll fade away." Alma's voice softened. "I think that's why he came to you."

Tuomas frowned. "What about Grandma?"

Alma let out a snort. "Irma doesn't believe in anything that can't be proven with a bank statement. She says Jaska doesn't exist—but she spends her nights watching movies about aliens, zombies, and vampires. What nonsense!"

At that very moment, something hissed in Tuomas' ear: "Speak of the devil..."

And just then, as if summoned, Irma Arkko glided out of the house in a long white dress and a broad-brimmed hat.

"Is Alma ready today?" she asked in a clipped tone, as if reading from a list.

"We just came from therapy," Alma replied.

"Therapy…" Irma's lip curled slightly. "Doesn't seem to have made much difference."

"It's only just begun," Alma said evenly.

"Does Alma need anything from town?" Irma asked, though her voice betrayed little genuine concern.

"Tuomas needs a swimsuit. When the lake warms up, we'll start water therapy," Alma replied with forced cheerfulness.

Irma raised an eyebrow. "So now Alma's the boy's full-time therapist? Who's paying for this? Am I going to need a new kitchen assistant?"

Alma's eyes flashed, but her voice stayed calm. "Tuomas is family. Just like the lady of the house. So everything falls under household expenses. And as far as my work goes—it's been done faithfully for forty years. But since you brought it up… maybe it's time for a raise. Life's more expensive than it used to be."

Irma muttered something under her breath, turned, and disappeared into the garage.

Tuomas blinked. "Is she always like that?"

"Most of the time," Alma said lightly. "But it doesn't matter."

Just then, the same raspy voice whispered again: "Swamp there, quagmire here… black flanks on both sides."

Tuomas jumped. "That's him again!"

Alma smiled knowingly. "He's getting more comfortable with you."

"What does he look like?" Tuomas asked, his curiosity piqued.

Alma shrugged. "He changes. Some say he's like an elf. Others see him in the shape they imagine. Dwarves, gnomes… He once showed up in a Santa hat. He plays tricks, but he's never mean."

Tuomas thought about the hands that had caught him.

If that was Jaska… maybe he really wasn't alone here after all.

"But elves only exist in fairy tales," Tuomas said skeptically.

"You might think so," Alma replied with a mysterious smile, "but Jaska is real."

Tuomas shrugged. "It would be nice to see Jaska."

A soft hiss echoed in his ear, followed by a humming whisper: "You shouldn't judge a cat by its fur."

Tuomas looked up—there it was. The black cat with glowing red eyes and a silver nose ring was sitting on the porch steps again, tail curled neatly around its paws.

Tuomas couldn't help but laugh. "That's not Jaska, is it?"

"I'm afraid so," Alma confirmed.

"But he can't be the one who caught me before—I mean, look at him. No hands."

Alma chuckled. "You'd be surprised what he can do."

She turned to the cat. "Take care of Tuomas, Jaska. Don't let him fall and hurt himself again. You two can train together."

The cat gave a slow blink, stretched, mewed softly, and vanished without a sound.

With Irma off in town for the day, Tuomas decided to explore the house alone. The library, with its thick carpet and dust-muffled silence, seemed like the safest place. Two walls were lined with towering bookcases filled with faded spines and heavy tomes. The air smelled of old paper and beeswax.

He spotted some large photo albums on a lower shelf and pulled one out, settling cross-legged on the floor. The photos were all black and white—wedding portraits, posed family gatherings, solemn-looking children in stiff clothes. He found a picture of his grandparents' wedding, and one of his father as a smiling boy in knickerbockers. But there were no photos of Irma's side of the family.

Lost in time, Tuomas jumped when the door opened.

"There you are!" Alma said, her voice half scolding, half amused. "You could have called me if you needed help."

"I just wanted to look at the old photos," Tuomas explained.

Alma moved quickly to collect the albums. "Your grandmother doesn't like anyone poking through her things."

"But they're just pictures of Dad and Grandpa. Nothing secret. There aren't even any photos of Grandma's family."

Alma hesitated, then glanced toward the hallway. "That's... because your grandmother is ashamed of where she comes from. Her family was poor—her parents worked here as farmhands. When she married into the Arkko family, she had the old cottage torn down. Luckily, her parents had already moved away. Now come on, out of here before she gets back."

That evening, Irma returned in a flurry of perfume and dramatic flair. She swept into the kitchen, dressed in a crisp white dress with a matching scarf and belt in icy steel-blue. Her freshly dyed hair shimmered in the overhead light.

"What do you think, Alma?" she asked, spinning with an exaggerated pose.

"Very chic!" Tuomas blurted before Alma could answer.

Irma turned and gave him a genuine smile for the first time. "Ah, the young man has taste."

Then she vanished into the hall, leaving behind a trail of perfume—and the unmistakable scent of red wine.

"She went back to the restaurant again," Alma muttered. "Spent money like water. And forgot your bathing suit, of course."

As Midsummer approached, Tuomas' father promised to return for the celebration. Tuomas wanted to surprise him —he was determined to walk without crutches by then. Each day, he practiced in secret, and each day, Jaska was there.

At first, invisible arms held him under the arms, steadying him. Later, Jaska only lightly touched his elbow. Eventually, Tuomas managed to walk across the yard from the manor steps to the old attic stairwell—almost alone.

Jaska retrieved the crutches Tuomas had left behind and set them quietly beside him. Then he sat down next to the boy, invisible but unmistakably present.

By now, Tuomas didn't need to see Jaska. He could feel him—like static in the air, a faint warmth at his side.

"Tell me more," Tuomas whispered. "About the other creatures. Are there really others like you?"

Jaska's reply didn't come in words. Instead, thoughts swirled in Tuomas' mind—images, memories, and impressions that weren't his own. It felt like thoughts bouncing between two mirrors. Quick, wordless. A game of mental ping-pong.

He laughed aloud. If only talking to people was this easy.

Jaska's thoughts came through like flashes:

Once, the Arkko estate had been full of spirits. House elves, sauna guardians, granary keepers, mill spirits. Each had their job—protecting, watching, helping.

"I used to be a mill elf," came the whisper in Tuomas' head, tinged with pride. "But then..."

The thought faded, heavy with sadness.

"But then, no more grain. No more cattle. The mill stopped turning. The sauna grew cold. No one believed anymore. So... they disappeared. Like snow melting in a spring crevice."

Tuomas felt a twinge of guilt. "But you stayed?"

"Alma kept me here. She believed. She remembered."

"Are there others like you anywhere?" Tuomas asked.

"In the old church," Jaska answered. "It was built from salvaged mansions—places where spirits once lived. They're still there, hidden in rafters and bell towers. And on the other side of the bay, on Teufelsberg... strange things crawl there. Not elves. More like little devils."

Tuomas shivered. "And how long have you lived here?"

"Longer than anyone can count," came the answer. "As long as the manor itself."

Tuomas sat very still on the step beside the invisible presence, his heart full of wonder.

In this old house, full of stern ancestors and forgotten traditions, Tuomas had found something no one else had: a friend.

19

As promised, Tuomas' father, Olli, returned to Arkko Manor for Midsummer. He had called the night before, shortly after landing at Helsinki Airport.

"I brought you something nice. I'll see you tomorrow," he'd said.

"I don't need anything. But maybe you could bring my swimsuit from home—if it still fits. Alma wants to take me swimming after Midsummer," Tuomas had replied.

The next morning, the house was buzzing with preparations. Alma insisted on celebrating properly, just like in the old days. Olli hadn't been home for Midsummer in years, and for Tuomas, it was the first time.

In the kitchen, Alma bustled around in a red apron and matching headscarf. She baked Karelian pies, and cinnamon buns—korvapuusti as the locals called them. Tuomas learned how to crimp the dough edges of the Karelian pies at the table. He loved brushing the cinnamon buns with egg wash and sprinkling them with sugar.

But something bugged him: the sugar never stuck well to the curved tops. Then an idea struck—he filled a bowl with sugar crystals, dipped a bun in it, and gave it a twist. The sugar stuck evenly all over.

"Now that's going to be delicious," he grinned.

"You could be a baker, you know," Alma said, impressed. "I've been baking my whole life, and I never thought of that."

Still warm from the oven, the sticky buns tasted even better with a glass of cold milk. The caramelied sugar stuck to the roof of his mouth—but that only made them more satisfying. The Karelian pies, however, needed to rest. Alma dipped them in a hot milk-butter mixture and layered them in a bowl, covering them with paper and a thick towel.

"Otherwise, they'll be hard as shoe soles," she explained.

Alma looked almost elfin as she danced around the kitchen. Tuomas had never seen her so happy. But the cheerful mood broke like glass when Irma suddenly swept into the room.

She glanced at Tuomas' hands, dusty with flour, then at the cinnamon buns cooling on the rack.

"Are the gentlemen now being trained in the arts of the kitchen maid?" she asked dryly.

"The arts of the kitchen maid have always pleased the gentlemen of this house," Alma replied without turning around.

Irma muttered something under her breath and left with a swirl of perfume.

"Why is Grandma so angry with you?" Tuomas asked quietly.

"Irma—your grandmother—has her reasons. But I can't always help that," Alma said with a sigh. "She's been difficult since she was young. But she wouldn't last a day in this house without me."

Tuomas felt relieved. At least Alma was irreplaceable here.

When Olli finally pulled into the yard after lunch, the outdoor table was already laid with all the delicacies he remembered from childhood: Karelian pies slathered with egg butter, herring and mushroom salad, crisp-fried vendace, and new potatoes. A strawberry cake with whipped cream sat on a side table.

Irma hadn't appeared all morning, but she'd been eavesdropping from the parlor. At the sound of car doors, she stepped onto the terrace with practiced elegance. Olli kissed her on the cheek.

"How long are you staying this time?" she asked at once.

"Two weeks," he replied. "But Tuomas and I might do a little traveling—depends how he's doing."

Tuomas beamed. A trip with Dad! Olli crouched to embrace him, holding him carefully, as if afraid his son might still break.

"Well, young man. How's it going?"

"Really well. Jaska has—" Tuomas began, but Olli quickly covered his mouth and glanced toward Irma.

"We'll talk about that later," he whispered.

The table looked magical. Alma had arranged midsummer roses and lilacs in a large vase, and scattered more lilac blossoms across the white cloth.

Tuomas felt a pang of guilt that Alma didn't join them at the table. She ate alone in the kitchen, as always.

During the meal, Olli talked about his travels—Tokyo, Dubai, Cape Town. "You should travel too, Mom," he said to Irma. "Take a spa weekend in Estonia."

"Why would I go alone?"

"There'll be other guests. Take Alma with you—she's never traveled."

Irma laughed coldly. "Alma? I'd be ashamed."

Tuomas clenched his fork. Good thing Alma couldn't hear that, he thought bitterly.

After dessert, Olli stood and stretched. "Let's see what I've got for you in the car."

From the back seat, he carefully lifted out a brand-new bicycle. It gleamed in the afternoon sun—multiple gears, shiny fenders.

"Vacation's a good time to practice," Olli said. "We didn't want you biking in Helsinki traffic."

Tuomas' eyes widened. It was beautiful.

"But you'll need your energy tonight. The midsummer celebration at the harbor could go late."

"Will you be okay getting up to your room by yourself?" Olli asked. "I need to talk to Alma."

Tuomas nodded, but curiosity got the better of him. He followed quietly, staying just outside the kitchen door.

"Well, Alma," Olli said, "has the boy been a handful?"

"Of course not," Alma said. Then her voice dropped. "But there's something I need to tell you. The money didn't stretch far enough. I had to pay for the whitefish myself."

"What? I've been transferring five hundred euros a month to Irma—for Tuomas' meals."

"I haven't seen a cent more than usual. And even that I have to beg for. Irma spends on clothes and restaurants, but I get reminders about my wages. Your father, for all his faults, had the finances under control. He promised me a raise before he left for Thailand."

Olli's voice grew sharper. "That's a serious accusation."

"I'm not complaining," Alma said. "She's your mother. But I never trusted her. And with good reason. Something was off from the beginning."

"Now you're exaggerating," Olli muttered. "What do you mean?"

Alma looked at him squarely. "You were too young to notice. But the rest of us saw it."

"I don't think you and Seijaliisa had the same father," Alma said quietly. "There was a lot of gossip back then. Even though she was born only five months after the wedding, she wasn't a premature baby. I saw her with my own eyes."

"Alma, watch what you're saying!" Olli snapped. "That's a serious accusation."

"I'm not saying it matters now. But someone needs to take control of things around here—especially for Tuomas' sake. Just don't bring this up with your mother, or she'll sulk for weeks."

Olli said nothing more and left the kitchen. As he stepped into the library, voices echoed down the hallway—sharp, raised, and unmistakably angry.

Memories of his father flickered in his mind.

Heikki Arkko had studied agriculture but had little interest in working the land. The Arkko estate, once prosperous with cattle, fields, and forest, had been steadily hollowed out. While the estate brought in a decent income, Heikki preferred horse racing and gambling to farming. When he drowned in the Thailand tsunami, Olli had returned home to settle the estate, only to uncover an unpleasant surprise: most of the fields had been leased away, and valuable waterfront land had been sold to developers building vacation homes.

All that remained were dilapidated buildings, a few patches of forest, and a will that gave Olli legal ownership—but left Irma the right to live in and manage the property.

In theory, she was responsible for all expenses in exchange for staying in the manor house. But when Olli tried to review the finances, Irma brushed him off with claims that everything was handled by an accounting office in town.

Yet now, in a neat stack on the desk by the window, he spotted several overdue utility bills. They were stamped in red: PAYMENT NOTICE.

"Mom," he said, struggling to keep calm, "do you realize the electricity's about to be shut off if these bills aren't paid?"

"I'll get the money," Irma replied flatly. "Don't worry."

"From where?"

"I'm selling a piece of shoreline. We're not building on it."

"You're out of your mind! The shore's the most valuable thing left!"

"You have money," Irma snapped. "Life insurance from your father, his widow's pension, and the lease payments. Don't act like feeding two old women is such a burden."

"Unbelievable," Olli muttered. "The apartment in the city doesn't need renovations. This place—this crumbling ruin—should be torn down. But no, it's 'historically protected.' And the central heating?"

"It hasn't worked in years."

"You never told me!"

"Because you stopped caring a long time ago. You don't care about this house—or the people in it."

Olli took a deep breath. "Fine. Monday morning, I'm making appointments with the bank. I'll handle it."

He left the room, jaw tight, pulse pounding.

Later, he found Tuomas resting in his room. The boy looked up as he entered, setting aside a book with an old leather cover.

"You wanted to tell me about Jaska," Olli said, sitting down on the edge of the bed. "Have you... met him?"

Tuomas nodded. "Yeah. We've had a few chats."

Olli gave a quiet laugh. "He's something else. Shame you can't understand half of what he says."

"You have to... sort of feel what he means. It's not exactly talking."

"That sounds even harder."

Tuomas hesitated. His father didn't get it. Not really. He didn't understand that Jaska's thoughts arrived like little sparks, instant and wordless. Not like people. People fumbled and spoke around the truth. Jaska just sent it.

And in that moment, Tuomas knew he couldn't explain it—couldn't explain how his own mind seemed to work differently now, after the accident. If he tried, would his father think something had gone wrong in his brain?

So Tuomas just gave a small, unreadable smile and looked away.

20

That evening, Olli and Tuomas headed to the Midsummer celebration at the village beach. Though it was only a fifteen-minute walk, Tuomas wouldn't have made it on foot —and truthfully, he enjoyed being back in his father's luxurious car.

Despite Tuomas' progress, his father insisted he bring the crutches. "Just in case," he'd said.

As they approached the beach, cars were parked in long rows along the roadside. A security guard flagged them down, motioning for Olli to turn around and park farther away.

"Unfortunately, I need to drive all the way down," Olli explained, holding up the crutches. "My son can't walk that far."

The guard studied the boy in the passenger seat, then nodded. "All right. Go ahead." He scribbled something and stuck a permit beneath the windshield wiper: Handicapped Transport.

Tuomas saw it as he got out. The words stung. He hated the label. Still, no one here knew him, and the crowd swallowed them up. He leaned on his crutches with extra emphasis—if people were going to stare, at least the explanation was clear. Officially handicapped, he thought bitterly. Words like cripple, lame, and invalid swirled in his mind.

A few hundred people had gathered on the beach. Families drifted between stands, eating sausages, sipping coffee from paper cups, and nibbling on pastries. At the edge of the fairgrounds, a gleaming red fire truck drew a line of excited kids. Little boys were hoisted into the cab, their faces glowing with joy.

"Want to check it out?" Olli asked, gesturing to the truck.

"I'm not a little kid," Tuomas said coolly. "Even if I'm... disabled."

But the truck was fascinating. It gleamed like a candy apple, and something in Tuomas stirred—something old and warm. Fire had nearly taken him once, but he couldn't remember the pain. Only the silence that followed.

Out on the water, a raft stacked with wood waited to become the midsummer bonfire. It floated safely offshore, a precaution against the unusually dry summer. Fires had already been banned in other regions.

As they neared the stand of the local Women's Association, Olli stopped abruptly. Tuomas looked up and followed his gaze to the woman behind the table.

"Anneli?" Olli asked, blinking. "You're back in Arvola?"

The woman's smile didn't reach her eyes. "Look who's graced us with his presence. Mr. von Arkko himself."

"Oh, come on. You left first. When did you move back?"

"I've been here for eight years. It's better for my daughter."

Tuomas peered around her and spotted a familiar face. "Miranda! You're here?"

A blonde girl stood behind the table, smiling nervously. "That's right. I'm helping my mom."

"She's visually impaired," Anneli said. "It's fine to say she's blind. It's the truth."

"But she reads really well—in that special book," Tuomas said. "With the dots. What's it called?"

"Braille," Miranda answered, turning her face toward his voice. "Are you Tuomas?"

"Yep. I'm the new student. This is my dad, Olli."

Miranda smiled again—strange, knowing. Nearby, older women whispered and exchanged glances. One woman approached, hand outstretched.

"Remember me? Aino Koskinen. You were in Reijo's class."

Olli shook her hand. "Reijo, yes! He and I got into all kinds of trouble together."

Aino's expression dimmed. "He drove his snowmobile into the lake three years ago. Thin ice."

"That sounds like Reijo," Olli said, somber. "Always going too fast. I'm sorry for your loss."

Tuomas noticed one of the women glance from Miranda to his father. Her lips barely moved: "Is he...?" and again, quieter, "Like father and..."

Before the whisper could spread, Anneli raised her voice.

"Ladies, anyone interested in natural pest control? We've got brochures—samples too!"

The women shuffled away, murmuring, embarrassed.

"Come on, Tuomas," Olli said, gently tugging his son along. "Maybe we'll see them again later."

He found a bench near the water's edge and helped Tuomas sit, then disappeared to get them sausages. Tuomas sat alone, watching the crowd, until three boys stopped in front of him.

"Well, look who flew in—the red woodpecker," sneered Mirko, the long-haired boy from class. "Good thing the fire truck's here, in case your hair goes up in flames."

Laughter from the others.

Tuomas flushed, but before he could react, his father returned, handing him a paper tray with a steaming sausage.

"Making friends?" Olli asked.

"Not exactly," Tuomas muttered, chewing without enthusiasm.

The sun was just beginning to dip toward the horizon when a hush fell over the crowd. A small boat rowed toward the floating raft. The rower lit a torch and tossed it onto the dry pile. Smoke rose first, then flame—a golden tongue licking skyward, erupting into a blazing tower.

Cheers broke out. Sparks floated above the lake. But then, silence.

Even the children. All eyes turned toward the fire, its reflection flickering on the black water.

Tuomas felt something stir in his chest. Something ancient and wordless. The fire felt alive, like a presence from long ago—comforting and terrifying at once.

He leaned forward slightly, mesmerized. Would he have stepped into it if it had burned on land? Would he have let the flames consume him?

A wave of dizziness passed through him. He closed his eyes.

In the crackling silence, he felt it again—something pulling him, whispering without words.

21

The following night, Tuomas woke to a noise—a sharp clatter beside his bed. One of the crutches had fallen to the floor. The other was... floating. It hovered in the air, slowly drifting toward the door, which had creaked open as if by invisible hands.

Tuomas sat up, blinking in disbelief.

"Jaska! How dare you? Bring back the crutch!"

But the crutch had already disappeared into the hallway.

Without hesitating, Tuomas grabbed the remaining crutch, hoisted himself upright, and limped after it. When he reached the hall, he saw the crutch now gliding across the terrace, illuminated by the soft glow of the midsummer night. It wasn't quite dark—more like an eerie, golden dusk. The sun still hovered on the edge of the sky, reluctant to disappear.

Across the yard, near the garages, Tuomas spotted movement. Three men were creeping around his father's car.

One was fiddling with the lock on the driver's door. Another had already unhooked Tuomas's brand-new bike from the wall and was examining the gears. The third leaned casually against the car, smoking, eyes darting between his companions.

Tuomas stood frozen, heart hammering.

Then came a sudden yelp.

The bike thief dropped the bicycle like it had burned him. "Ow! What the hell? Who hit me?"

"Nobody hit anybody," said the smoker.

Another yelp cut him off. The man at the car door jerked and collapsed, clutching his backside.

"What's happening?" he shouted. "Someone just walloped me! My shoulder—damn it, my collarbone!"

The men spun around just in time to see the floating crutch hovering menacingly in midair. It was slowly circling them like a shark in still water.

"Dude… this place is haunted," one of them stammered.

"We need to get out of here. Now."

"But I can't drive—my arm's busted," moaned the first.

"My shoulder's wrecked," groaned another.

"I don't even have a license," the third added weakly.

"Doesn't matter—just get us out of here!"

They scrambled toward their car, parked at the end of the oak-lined lane. But before they could escape, the car shuddered violently.

CRACK! The rear window exploded. The side mirrors twisted off like paper.

The men dove inside, slamming the doors. The unlicensed driver fumbled with the ignition. The engine roared to life—but the car didn't budge.

"Let go of the brake!"

"I did!"

"Put it in first, you idiot!"

"I am in first! It won't move!"

Then, as if some invisible force finally let go, the car lurched forward like a wild animal breaking free. The men screamed as it shot down the road, disappearing into the woods, tail lights bouncing.

Back in the yard, a single crutch floated peacefully in the air, along with a torn license plate that twirled slowly like a leaf on the breeze.

Jaska glided back across the lawn and presented the crutch to Tuomas like a knight returning a stolen sword.

Tuomas laughed, breathless. "Thank you, Jaska! You saved my bike—and Dad's car. You're amazing! But… what are you going to do with the license plate?"

Jaska hummed an old melody—a sad, lilting tune that Tuomas didn't recognie, but somehow understood. Then, with his usual cryptic flair, he whispered:

"Your memory is dear to me when there's nothing else left…"

Tuomas raised an eyebrow, smirking. "Let me guess—you think a car without a license plate and full of dents might attract some attention?"

The crutch bobbed once in what looked suspiciously like a nod.

"Not the first time this old manor attracted trouble, huh?" Tuomas added. "Let me guess—there are more license plates under the windmill?"

Jaska didn't answer. But somewhere, under the floorboards of the old mill, the wind stirred… and metal whispered against metal.

22

The next morning, Olli entered the kitchen early, before the rest of the house had stirred. He found Alma already at work, slicing bread and preparing coffee.

"So, did you enjoy the party last night?" she asked looking up.

"The program wasn't much," Olli replied, reaching for a cup. "But did you know Anneli Mattila is living in Arvola again?"

Alma paused. "You saw her?"

"We talked."

She gave a small smile. "You had a bit of a thing for her back in the day, didn't you?"

"Maybe," Olli said, brushing it off. "But Anneli left before I did."

"She had her reasons," Alma murmured. "At least, that's what people said."

"What reasons?" Olli asked, suddenly attentive.

"She came back with a blind child. Helps her parents with the house now. Can't really take outside jobs—she has to get the girl to and from school."

Olli sighed. "A shame. She was always such a bright girl."

"Pretty, too," Alma added. Then she glanced sideways. "Probably a genetic defect."

Her tone was light, but Olli felt a flicker of unease.

At breakfast in the dining room, the tension from yesterday's argument between Irma and Olli still lingered like smoke after a fire. Tuomas, caught in the middle, tried to break the silence.

"Alma bakes really good bread," he said cautiously.

Irma gave a curt nod. "After all these years, I suppose she's learned a thing or two." Then, after a beat, she softened slightly. "So... how was the party? Did you meet any friends?"

"Only a few," Olli replied. "Anneli Mattila was there with her daughter. Tuomas will apparently be in her class this fall."

Irma choked on a piece of bread and coughed hard. She didn't say another word for the rest of the meal.

After clearing the table, Olli clapped his hands together. "Let's try out your new bike," he said to Tuomas with a smile.

He wheeled the bicycle from the garage into the hallway and helped Tuomas into the saddle. "Let's see if the height works for you. Don't worry—I'll hold on."

Tuomas had learned to ride a bike back in La Colombaia. First on Chiara's pink girl's bike, then on Guido's battered men's bike with no gears and only a backpedal brake. He wasn't afraid of the mechanics—but after months in recovery, his legs still weren't strong. Pushing the pedals was like trying to stir concrete.

They rode slowly down the long oak-lined avenue, the trees arching overhead in a bright green tunnel. To the right, a narrow path cut through fields of ripening grain.

"I think that's barley," Olli said, squinting. "Or wheat. Could be oats. Maybe rye?" He laughed. "As you can see, farming knowledge doesn't run in the family. I'm just a city farmer."

"Can we visit the mill?" Tuomas asked.

He had only seen the windmill from his bedroom window. Up close, it was enormous—taller and more imposing than he'd imagined. The blades alone stretched like arms toward the sky.

"The mill has two parts," Olli explained. "The base is cone-shaped—like a wide skirt. That's why it's called a 'mamsell mill.' The top section, where the blades are, can be rotated to face the wind."

He took a heavy iron key from his jacket pocket and fitted it into the old wooden door. It creaked open with a groan, and the smell of old grain and flour dust enveloped them like a memory.

Inside, the space was a maze of wooden platforms, stairs, and massive interlocking beams. Wheels and pulleys filled the air with the silence of dormant motion.

"How did anyone keep track of all this?" Tuomas whispered.

"The miller was a real craftsman," Olli said. "He learned everything from the previous generation. Usually father to son—kind of like royalty, passing down a crown."

"Could you have worked here?" Tuomas asked, glancing around in awe.

Olli shook his head. "I never learned enough. The grain went into those big hoppers, then down between the stones. The blades outside turned the whole thing. But... I never saw it working. Maybe only one person still knows."

"Who?" Tuomas asked, though he already suspected the answer.

Olli smiled faintly. "Jaska. Do you think he's still around?"

Tuomas shrugged, hiding a grin. He didn't want to say he'd seen Jaska—at least in the form of a black cat with red eyes and a nose ring—slip beneath the mill just a few days ago. Maybe Jaska still held a grudge, he thought. Maybe he was just waiting.

In the following days, Tuomas riding every morning. At first, Olli held tightly to the back of the bike. Then, gradually, he let go. Tuomas pedaled alone—wobbly, determined.

But even when his father wasn't behind him, Tuomas never felt alone.

He could feel Jaska. Watching. Supporting. Always near.

23

Although nearly everyone in Finland—officials and businessmen alike—vanished summer vacation after the Midsummer Festival, Olli Arkko somehow managed to secure a bank appointment to sort out the estate's tangled finances.

When he returned from the city, he went straight to the kitchen to fetch Alma. Together, they entered the library where Irma was already waiting. Tuomas, who had been loitering in the hallway, pressed his ear to the door.

His father's voice was calm and steady, just like the announcements Tuomas imagined him making in the cockpit: "Dear passengers, we've now reached ten thousand meters…" Irma, on the other hand, sounded flustered. At one point, it even sounded like she was crying. Alma's voice was low, almost resigned: "Leave everything as it is."

Tuomas hurried back to his room just before the conversation ended.

When Olli entered, Tuomas sat up and asked bluntly, "What did you argue about?"

"We didn't argue exactly," Olli said, removing his jacket. "But your grandmother gets upset easily these days. The good news is, Alma will now get her salary paid directly into her own account. She won't have to ask Grandma for money anymore."

"That's great," Tuomas said. "Alma hates asking."

"Exactly. It'd be easiest for her to use online banking. I could get her a computer. Do you think you could teach her how to use it?"

Tuomas brightened. "Sure, I'll try."

From then on, all the bills for the estate were automatically paid through the account. Only Alma had access to the one set aside for Tuomas' care.

Irma was furious.

"You trust a stranger more than your own mother?" she snapped.

"That's right," Olli replied without hesitation.

Irma burst into tears.

When she threatened to sell more land, Olli warned her that he would have her declared legally incompetent if she made another move without consulting him.

Lunch that day was quiet, stiff with tension. Irma picked at her food. Alma said little. Tuomas, trying his best to cut through the silence, looked at his father.

"Dad, you promised we'd go on a trip together."

Irma snorted. "Go ahead. Leave us alone."

Before Olli could respond, his phone rang. He stepped out into the hallway to take the call.

When he returned, his face had changed.

"I'm sorry, Tuomas. I have to go back to work. There's a stomach virus going around—half the crew is sick. And it's peak tourist season."

Tuomas stared at his plate. "So we're not going?"

"We'll have to postpone," Olli said gently. "But I'll get extra vacation days in the fall. We'll make it up then."

Tuomas was crushed. As if the planes wouldn't stay in the air without his father!

"Then can you at least take me to La Colombaia?" he asked, desperate for a different answer.

"I can't," Olli said, clearly uncomfortable. "The stairs are too steep for you right now, and Chiara still has school. She's helping out in the restaurant. It's not a good time."

Of course not. No one had time for Tuomas.

Chiara was already being groomed to take over the family business. She had a purpose. Tuomas had crutches.

That same evening, Olli packed his suitcase. Before he left, he hugged Tuomas tightly at the doorway.

"I'm really sorry, son. Summer's just getting started. We'll still have time to do fun things—okay?"

Tuomas didn't answer. He stood stiffly, arms at his sides.

He was angry. Disappointed. And underneath it all— deeply sad.

He only had one person left in the world. And even his father didn't seem to have time for him.

24

The next day, Alma noticed how quiet and withdrawn Tuomas was. "How about we go to the beach today?" she suggested. "The shore there is nice and shallow, and the water warms up quickly. You can swim, can't you?"

Tuomas nodded. Of course he'd been in swimming pools before—but never in a lake, where fish and crabs and leeches swam freely. He couldn't tell Alma that. She'd only laugh. A Finnish boy, afraid of the lake? What a disgrace.

After finishing her morning chores, Alma packed juice and sandwiches into a cooler bag. Tuomas had barely touched breakfast. She took his crutches too, just in case, though she believed he could make it to the water without them. At her suggestion, he'd already put on his swimsuit under his jeans so he wouldn't have to deal with the changing rooms.

Alma brought only a large blanket, saying she didn't plan to swim.

The beach was nestled in a quiet bay of soft, fine sand. A long wooden jetty stretched out into the deeper water where older kids cannonballed into the lake. The summer break had just begun, and the beach was crowded with families. Tuomas frowned when he spotted Mirko and his gang at the far end of the jetty. As usual, they were acting like they owned the place—running back and forth, shoving smaller kids aside, sending them tumbling into the lake whether they could swim or not.

Alma spread the blanket in the shade of a silver willow and lay back with a contented sigh.

"You'll be fine on your own, won't you?" she said, closing her eyes.

Tuomas stripped down to his swimsuit and placed his clothes neatly beside Alma's blanket. His skin looked painfully pale under the early summer sun, and he hesitated, glancing around. Young mothers kept watch over children digging sandcastles and racing with buckets between water and shore. Teen girls lay stretched out on colorful towels, adjusting sunglasses, watching for boys.

Tuomas walked slowly to the water's edge. It felt icy. But he knew people were watching, so he didn't stop. He kept going until the water reached his chest. After the first shock passed, it was soothing—cool and alive, like a gentle embrace. He kicked his legs, moved his arms, and before long he was gliding through the water with ease.

Maybe I could jump off the jetty too, he thought.

He climbed out and headed toward the pier, where a crowd of his future classmates had gathered. Just as he reached the middle, someone shouted:

"Look! The red-headed woodpecker's come to wet his feathers!"

Laughter erupted. Mirko. Of course.

"Can the bird fly too?" Mirko jeered.

Without warning, Mirko charged from the base of the pier, sprinting straight at Tuomas. The others scrambled out of the way to avoid being shoved. Tuomas didn't move. Something deep within him rose up—an iron-willed force that refused to be bullied.

In his mind flashed the image of the kilometer stone at the end of the oak-lined road near the manor—a heavy slab of gray granite that weighed hundreds of kilos. Unmovable. Unbreakable.

Mirko's expression changed the instant he realized Tuomas wasn't flinching. But it was too late to stop. He slammed into something invisible.

He screamed in pain and stumbled backward, rolling across the pier before plunging into the water.

Everyone froze.

A moment later, a voice cried out from under the dock. "Help!"

Several boys dove in after him. Tuomas, calm as ever, walked to the end of the jetty, dove in, swam a lap, and returned to shore.

By the time he reached Alma's blanket, she had the sandwiches and drinks laid out. In the distance, Mirko was being helped ashore by his gang. His face was twisted in pain. A dark red mark was spreading across his belly— rectangular, with the number 31 and an arrow.

Why 31? Tuomas wondered.

Then it hit him. The old stone at the manor had 13 carved into it—the distance to the next town. The number had been mirrored onto Mirko's skin. But that was just in my head... Tuomas thought, chilled.

Had Jaska done it?

That evening, Tuomas asked him.

"Did you help me at the beach today?"

"Jaska can't go far. Jaska must stay close. If Jaska leaves, he disappears—like..." The voice paused.

"Like a fart in the Sahara?" Tuomas offered.

"Exactly!" Jaska giggled, high-pitched and strange.

Later that night, back in bed, Tuomas replayed it all in his mind.

How was that possible? If I imagined I was a kilometer stone... and I actually became one—am I still normal?

And then, more unsettling: Is it normal to talk to someone who isn't there? Or... someone only he could see?

25

Tuomas' leg muscles were growing stronger by the day, thanks to his daily bike training. Jaska still followed him like a loyal dog as he rode along the oak-lined avenue, but now he no longer needed to be pushed or supported. The therapist was so impressed with his progress that he considered recommending to Olli that they pause the therapy sessions—at least for now.

It looked like Tuomas would soon be able to ride to school on his own. The building was less than two kilometers from the Arkko farm, and there was a safe bike path leading straight there. Alma wouldn't have to drive him anymore—though she still teased him about it.

In the early mornings, Tuomas went swimming alone. He made sure to go before Mirko and his two sidekicks—the worst bullies in town—were even awake. When they did pass him by, they only shot him dirty looks and kept walking. But it was clear they were biding their time, waiting for a chance to get even.

Tuomas rarely saw his grandmother Irma that summer. She spent most days alone in the bedroom, the library, or the dining room. Sometimes she asked Alma to set up a lounge chair under the apple trees so she could recline in the shade with a stack of fashion magazines. Several times a week she drove into town and returned with shopping bags from expensive boutiques.

"What does she do with all those clothes? It's not like she gets visitors," Alma said once. "The villagers aren't good enough for her."

"Then she must be very lonely," Tuomas offered.

"That's her own fault."

Tuomas didn't miss his grandmother's company. He had Alma, Jaska, and his father, who called regularly over Skype. He was in the middle of one such call when Grandma suddenly appeared in his room.

"I have to go," Tuomas said quickly. "A visitor just came." He shut the laptop.

Irma sat down on the desk chair—just as Jaska scrambled out of the way and onto Tuomas' bed. Tuomas fought the urge to grin. What would she have said if she knew she'd nearly flattened the house elf?

"Have you been talking to your father?" she asked, her voice dry. She smelled faintly of cognac.

"Yes," Tuomas replied.

"So, you're starting school here in Arvola?"

"Yes."

"Do you even have proper clothes? Children from Arkko Manor don't go around in rags."

Her eyes swept disapprovingly over Tuomas' jeans, torn at the knees—a fashion statement she clearly didn't understand.

"My dad brought everything I need," he said. "Clothes, books—everything."

"Alma should double-check. Men are clueless. And she needs to take you to the hairdresser. You look like a girl with all that hair. Not that much can be done about the color." She stood, sighed, and left the room without another word.

On the first day of school, Tuomas spotted Miranda arriving with her mother. He also recognized a few other students—including, unfortunately, Mirko and his two ever-present "bodyguards," as Tuomas had come to call them.

In the classroom, the teacher—Paula Puntanen, known simply as Paula—placed Tuomas in the front row between Miranda and Mirko. Each student had their own desk, arranged flexibly to allow for group work.

Tuomas glanced at Mirko and stuck out his tongue. Mirko gave him a slow, threatening smile in return.

Just wait, Mirko seemed to say.

Tuomas ignored him. At least he'd gotten a haircut before school started, thanks to Alma. His short red hair looked clean and neat now—hopefully less of a target.

Word of the beach incident must have spread, because some students gave him curious, even wary looks. Tuomas tried to stay as low-profile as possible.

Everything went smoothly—until biology class that afternoon.

Paula opened with an announcement: "We'll be going to Susiniemi Camp this fall! There'll be hikes, outdoor lessons on mosses and mushrooms, and—"

The class erupted with cheers.

"Now," she continued, "let's get in the mood. Who can tell me—?"

Tuomas raised his hand.

"Yes, Tuomas? What would you like to ask?"

"Lily of the valley," he said.

"Excuse me?"

"Lily of the valley," he repeated, then added, "It's the national flower of Finland."

Paula blinked at him, startled. "How did you know I was about to ask that?"

There was a beat of silence—then the room exploded in laughter.

Paula banged her pointer on the desk to restore order. "All right, quiet down. Tuomas—how did you answer a question I hadn't even asked yet?"

Tuomas squirmed in his seat. What could he say? The question had just popped into his head, clear as day.

"It just… came to me," he mumbled.

"Well," Paula said after a pause, "that's very… remarkable. But please—try to wait until questions are actually asked before answering."

Tuomas nodded quickly, wishing he could disappear into the floor. Out of the corner of his eye, he saw Miranda smiling faintly. Somehow, that helped.

26

During the break, Tuomas retreated behind the tall pine trees at the edge of the schoolyard. After the embarrassing moment in biology class, he wanted to be alone. From his hiding spot, he watched Mirko and his usual crew lurking near the bike racks behind the school.

Suddenly, one of them grabbed Tuomas's brand-new bike. Grinning, the boys hauled it toward the woods— even though it was locked. They simply picked it up and dragged it away like scavengers claiming stolen prey.

With all the commotion of the first day, none of the teachers or students noticed what was happening. A narrow stream ran through a deep ditch not far from the school. The boys stopped at a small footbridge and exchanged looks that only spelled trouble. Then, with a triumphant smirk, Mirko hoisted the bike and hurled it over the railing into the water.

Tuomas saw it all from his hiding place. But he didn't move. He knew better now—there were other ways to handle this.

He felt it again—that strange, swelling power rising up from inside, just like it had on the pier. The boys deserved what was coming. If they were so obsessed with his bike, fine—let them keep it.

As the bike splashed into the ditch, something strange happened: Mirko couldn't let go. His hands were stuck to the handlebars, and he stumbled forward, dragged by the weight of the bike.

"Ow! What the hell?!" he yelled.

His sneaker slipped on a mossy rock, and he toppled headfirst into the water, bike and all. His friends doubled over in laughter from the bridge above.

"You morons! Sheep-heads!" Mirko spat. "I tripped!"

"Get out before someone sees!" one of the boys shouted.

"I can't!" Mirko hissed. "My fingers are stuck! They're cramped or something—pull me up!"

Matias clambered down into the ditch, grabbing Mirko's arm while Väinö anchored them both from the bridge. After a lot of yelling and tugging, they finally hauled Mirko out—soaked, furious, and still clutching the bike as if it had claimed him as its own.

"Satan's cramp!" Mirko cursed, dripping from head to toe.

"School's starting. We have to go, or the teachers'll notice," Väinö muttered, glancing nervously around.

"You're not leaving me like this!" Mirko snapped.

But it turned out none of them could leave. They were all stuck—literally. Mirko's right hand was fused to the handlebars, Matias's left hand was locked onto Mirko's arm, and Väinö's grip on Matias wouldn't release either.

To anyone watching, they looked like three best friends bound in a heartfelt, unbreakable pact—except for their panicked expressions.

Their strange parade—three boys and a bike—turned heads as they shuffled into the schoolyard. Students burst into laughter. A supervising teacher approached, eyes narrowed, then softened at the sight of drenched Mirko.

"What's going on here?" he asked, suspicious.

"Well... someone dumped the bike in the ditch," Matias said quickly. "We were just getting it back. Thought it might belong to a student."

"Good initiative," the teacher said. "But Mirko, you need to go home and change. You can't sit in class soaked like that—you'll catch a cold."

Mirko gritted his teeth as his friends helped him push the bike back to the rack. The moment the wheels locked into place, something shifted. Their hands released all at once—just like that.

The bell rang, and the students rushed into the building. Tuomas, one of the last to enter, casually inspected his bike. It was unharmed.

In class, Mirko's sidekicks kept glancing at Tuomas with uneasy eyes, but they couldn't make sense of what had happened. After all, Tuomas hadn't been anywhere near the ditch when it all unfolded.

Tuomas, however, was shaken. That force—whatever it was—had come over him again. This time, someone could've been seriously hurt. If Mirko had hit his head on a rock, if he'd drowned…

Tuomas shivered.

What is this power? Where does it come from?

He'd never believed in heaven or hell, but now he wondered: Was he possessed? Had something dark taken root in him? Surely this wasn't the work of angels. He'd already hurt people twice just by getting angry. What if next time… someone died?

If only I could talk to someone, he thought. But I can't tell Dad. He's already worried. Alma would just say I'm imagining things. Grandma's... not an option. The therapist, maybe? But I'm not even seeing him anymore.

The thought pressed down on him like a weight. If I don't talk to someone soon, I'm going to lose my mind.

27

After school, Tuomas went straight to the windmill. As if sensing his arrival, Jaska appeared almost instantly and settled beside him on the wide wooden steps. The elf didn't say anything at first, but Tuomas could feel that he already knew something was wrong. Even their usual wordless connection—the rapid, silent exchange of thoughts and feelings—felt clouded, blocked by something Tuomas himself couldn't quite name.

Finally, Jaska broke the silence with a sharp hiss.
"Spit it out, Tuomas. What's eating you?"

Tuomas hesitated. Then, quietly, he said, "I think... I might be crazy."

Jaska snorted. "Everyone is. More or less."

Tuomas looked up. "Do you believe in angels? Or devils?"

"What?" Jaska blinked. "Jaska's lived a long time. Only angels and devils I've seen are people. Some are both. Why do you ask a fool question like that?"

Tuomas drew in a long, shaky breath. And then it all spilled out—his fears, the strange force that surged through him when he was angry, how Mirko had been thrown back at the pier and then trapped by the bike. How it had happened again that day. Things no ordinary person could do. He told Jaska everything.

Jaska didn't interrupt. He listened, nodding, his eyes unusually serious.

When Tuomas finished, Jaska scratched his head thoughtfully. "Well, Jaska's never met a human who can talk to him like you can. That already makes you different.

But Jaska doesn't think you're a devil. Not even a small one."

"Then what am I?" Tuomas asked. "What if I'm... not really human?"

Jaska tapped his chin with a long, knobby finger. "What if... you're a goblin?"

Tuomas groaned. "That's all I need! No, thanks. I'm human."

Jaska grinned, but didn't press it. Even if he couldn't give Tuomas the answer he wanted, just saying the words out loud felt like a relief. Tuomas let out a long breath and leaned back against the sun-warmed wood.

After a while, he glanced at Jaska. "Hey... why do you always talk like that? Like you're a little kid? 'Jaska thinks this,' 'Jaska wants that.' Why not just say, 'I think' or 'I want'?"

"Because that's how it was," Jaska said with a shrug. "Back when the estate was full of people, the masters never called the servants by 'Mr.' or 'Mrs.' Just first names. Alma sweeps the floors. Jussi hitches the horse. Jaska minds the mill. That's how it went. You get used to talking like that, and then... well, you never really stop."

Tuomas frowned. "Is that because the masters thought they were better than everyone else?"

Jaska gave him a long look. "Maybe. Probably. But Jaska's used to it now."

"Well," Tuomas said slowly, "you're not a servant to me. Or less than me. You're a really good guy. A friend."

Jaska blinked. His nose twitched, and he wiped it on his sleeve. "No one's ever called Jaska a friend before."

Tuomas smirked. "Don't start crying or anything. Or I'll take it back."

Jaska chuckled, and for the first time all day, Tuomas felt something like peace.

28

No kid wants to be special—he just wants to be like everyone else. Tuomas was no different. All he wanted was to be a normal Finnish boy.

Luckily, no one could tell that he was only half-Finnish. His eyes weren't the rich chocolate brown of his mother's side of the family—the Italians from Sicily—but a clear sapphire blue, like many Finns. And though he didn't have the straw-blond hair common among his classmates, there were enough redheads in Finland for his fiery curls not to raise eyebrows.

No one at school or in the village knew that his mother had been Italian. His first name, Tuomas, was Finnish through and through—slightly old-fashioned, maybe, but old names were back in style. Boys in class were named Hugo, Eino, Onni. Girls went by Hilma, Helmi, or Sohvi. On paper, at least.

Still, as the weeks passed, Tuomas couldn't shake the feeling that he didn't quite belong. At school, in the village, everywhere—he was like a mismatched puzzle piece forced into place. Even his way of speaking set him apart. The slang from Helsinki, where he'd grown up, clashed with the local dialect of Arvola. And every time he opened his mouth, he felt it—that subtle shift in the air, the flicker of unspoken judgment in the minds of others. If he wanted, he could read them:

Ah, a city boy. From Helsinki. Not one of us.

At least he kept his temper in check. He hadn't lost control once. Not when someone grabbed his cap at recess and tossed it into a rowan tree, where it stayed for days until the wind finally blew it down. Not even when someone tripped him in the hallway. He said nothing. Just got up and kept walking.

Even the teasing about Miranda didn't get to him. "Tuomas is in love with the blind girl," they'd whisper, snickering behind their hands. But he never reacted. Because it wasn't like that. Yes, Miranda was beautiful, but Tuomas didn't think of her that way. He saw her more as someone to protect. And even that was probably unnecessary. She was stronger than anyone gave her credit for.

He admired her—truly admired her. The way she read books by running her fingers over tiny dots of raised print. How her pale blue eyes, though they saw nothing, still managed to express emotion: concentration, amusement, warmth. She never acted helpless, never asked for special treatment.

Everyone in the village knew Miranda and her mother. The girls weren't jealous of her, because Miranda didn't care about appearances—she never looked in a mirror, never flaunted her beauty, never even knew how she looked compared to the rest. And even the roughest boys steered clear of teasing her. No one wanted to be the kid who picked on the blind girl. How could you prank someone who couldn't even see it coming?

29

Arvola didn't have its own indoor pool. Since swimming was part of the physical education curriculum, two classes rode the bus every other week to the municipal pool in the nearby town. Tuomas loved those lessons. In the water, he could almost keep up with the other boys.

Unlike in the school gym, where he was sidelined more often than not. His therapist had made it clear: no climbing the ropes, no jumping off boxes, no hanging from wall bars. His bones had healed, but they were still fragile, and his muscles—softened by months of immobility— were only slowly regaining strength. The gym teacher usually had him sit on the bench while the others worked up a sweat. But in the water, Tuomas could stretch, glide, and move freely. He felt whole.

Before entering the pool, the students were told—over and over—to remove all jewelry and anything that might fall off and get sucked into the filters. Tuomas slipped off his watch and removed the stone pendant his Nonna had given him before he left Italy. He wrapped them both in a sock and stuffed it inside one of his sneakers. The pendant was more than a souvenir. He wore it even at night, tucked beneath his shirt, the smooth weight of it resting against his chest. It made him feel like someone still had his back.

After class, Tuomas returned to the locker room. His shoes were right where he'd left them, neatly lined up under the bench. The sock was still inside one—but only the watch remained. The pendant was gone.

"Who took my stuff?" Tuomas shouted, his voice echoing off the tile. The other boys looked at him, startled, then glanced at each other and shrugged.

"No one saw anything."

But Tuomas noticed Väinö sneaking sideways glances toward Mirko. That was all the confirmation he needed. Mirko. Of course. Who else would it be?

But how could he prove it? He couldn't just rifle through Mirko's bag. And telling a teacher would make him look like a tattletale. Furious and helpless, he searched the lockers, peeked under benches, even checked the shower stalls. Nothing.

That pendant was the only thing he had left of Nonna. His throat tightened.

The class gathered in the lobby to wait for the bus. Someone wrinkled their nose and said, "Something smells burnt."

A few others sniffed. "Yeah, what is that?"

"Hey—Mirko's pants are smoking!" someone shouted. "His butt's on fire!"

A roar of laughter broke out.

But Mirko wasn't laughing. "It burns! What the—what's burning me?" he cried, hopping around and slapping at the back of his pants. Thick smoke billowed out of his pocket.

Panicking, Mirko yanked off his pants and shook them furiously. Smoke poured out of the fabric. Suddenly, a small object flew from the pocket and clattered across the floor—Tuomas's pendant.

Mirko dove to grab it before anyone else could react. He scooped it into his hand—and screamed.

"Damn thing's burning me!"

He flung the stone across the lobby like it was molten lava. The boys froze, staring. A kid from the other class chuckled and stooped to grab it, only to drop it with a hiss.

"Ow! What is that thing? It's hot!"

One by one, the boys backed away. Tuomas stepped forward. The pendant was lying perfectly still on the floor, innocent as ever. He knelt, picked it up without hesitation, and slipped the cord back over his head. The stone settled against his skin—cool and familiar.

"What's going on here?" barked the teacher from behind. "Outside—double file! The bus is waiting!"

Nobody wanted to sit next to Mirko on the ride home. His pants still smelled like burnt plastic, and he sulked silently in the last row. Strangely, no one sat next to Tuomas either.

Fine by him. He leaned his head against the window and closed his eyes, his fingers lightly brushing the stone at his chest. It was cool again. Comforting. Alive.

30

The time had come for the fall school camp. Tuomas's class was headed to a remote peninsula for a week of forest excursions, mushroom collecting, and evening campfires. It was school in name only—though their textbooks came along for the ride, no one expected much. Four adults would be supervising: their classroom teacher, Paula Puntanen; Mia's mother, a certified nature guide; Miranda's mother; and Kai's grandfather, who had volunteered to manage the firewood supply.

Breakfasts and dinners would be cooked on site. Lunches came from the Arvola school kitchen, which had taken on the formidable task of accommodating every dietary need imaginable—vegetarian, vegan, gluten-free, dietary , and peanut-allergic. The grownups agreed it would've been impossible to handle meals otherwise.

The students had no illusions: four adults couldn't possibly keep them from sneaking in some screen time with smartphones, tablets, and laptops.

But they were wrong.

As the bus rumbled off the bumpy forest road and pulled into the gravel parking lot of the camp center, Ms. Puntanen and Mia's mother stood at the front and held out yellow garbage bags.

"Devices, please," Ms. Puntanen said briskly. "Phones, tablets, games—everything."

The protests were loud, dramatic, and short-lived. No one dared challenge Ms. Puntanen for long. Everyone knew she practiced karate in her spare time, competed in shooting tournaments, and went on long backpacking trips through Kuusamo with more gear than most could lift. Rumor had it she'd even enlisted for military service—only to quit because, at five feet tall, she got tired of asking taller recruits to grab things from high shelves.

Once the confiscated electronics were sealed and labeled, she addressed the group.

"We're in nature now. There's plenty to do here—no need for screens. If there's an emergency, you can use my phone. Your parents have my number. We're not on the moon—Arvola is just twelve kilometers away."

The students, a little stunned, carried their lighter packs and sleeping bags into the main lodge. Boys and girls had separate bunk rooms, while the adults split the remaining quarters—Grandpa Kuitunen in a cozy room by himself, and the three women sharing another.

In the common room, everyone gathered on wooden benches, the scent of pine and distant campfire in the air.

"During this camp," Ms. Puntanen announced, "we'll explore mushrooms and mosses. Let's begin. Who can name a mushroom?"

"The fly agaric!" someone shouted.

"It's poisonous, stupid!" another student yelled back.

That was the full extent of their collective mycological knowledge.

Clearly, there was much to learn.

The week's plan involved collecting specimens in the forest, examining them with magnifying glasses and microscopes, comparing them with pictures in encyclopedias, and recording findings in worksheets. Ms. Puntanen and Mia's mother would lead the forest expeditions. Miranda's mother and Grandpa Kuitunen would remain behind, managing camp logistics and preparing meals.

Before the first foray into the woods, Mia's mother gathered the students under a large spruce tree.

"Think of yourselves as detectives on a manhunt," she said, her voice bright with enthusiasm. "First, you have to suspect. Then, you capture it—gently—and identify it. What's the skin like? Light? Mottled? Does it smell? Is it hairy? What shape is the cap—funnel, round, flat, wrinkled? What do the feet look like? Thick? Skinny?"

The children laughed, but listened closely.

"There are thousands of mushrooms in Finland," she continued, "and I hope you'll meet at least a few this week. But remember—don't yank them from the ground. Twist gently. The mycelium underground feeds the forest trees, and the trees give sugar to the mushrooms. It's a strange kind of friendship—but a vital one."

Miranda, who was blind, stayed behind that day, resting on a blanket under the trees. She listened as the others moved out into the underbrush with baskets and clipboards in hand.

By the time they returned, their baskets were brimming with specimens. The loot was carefully dumped onto outdoor tables, and the first real challenge began: identification.

The students hadn't expected it to be so hard. Was the cap bell-shaped or flat? Did it have gills, spines, or tubes underneath? Was there any milky sap when cut—and if so, what color? White, yellow, orange?

The mushroom books were opened, pages turning frantically.

What began as scientific work soon devolved into laughter.

"Väinö is a bottle mushroom!" someone shouted. "So round!"

"You're a cow's mouth!" came the retort.

"Tuomas is a reddish mushroom!" another yelled, pointing.

The forest had barely begun to work its spell—but already, the camp was off to an unforgettable start.

That turn of events had been inevitable. With learning behind them, the class dissolved into laughter and silliness.

The mushroom names were just too funny. Giddy chaos broke out across the room as students shouted bizarre Finnish words and playfully hurled them at one another.

Sensing the moment, Ms. Puntanen clapped her hands. "All right," she said. "Each table group: write down the five funniest mushroom names you can find in the guide—and one ridiculously long one. Ice cream goes to the winners."

She had never seen her students so enthusiastic about a class task. Pages flew as guides were flipped with wild intensity. Laughter echoed as pencils scribbled down outlandish names, and chatter bounced back and forth like ping pong balls in a hurricane.

Fifteen minutes later, the verdicts were in.

One by one, each group read their chosen names aloud. The competition was fierce, but in the end, the names were so absurd and equally entertaining that no clear winner could be chosen.

So everyone got ice cream.

The longest name turned out to be Suippumyrkkyseitikki—Cortinarius speciosissimus.

"Looks pretty. Orange-red. Smells like nothing, tastes like nothing—but it's deadly poisonous," Ms. Puntanen explained, pointing at the photo.

A collective gasp rippled through the group. Everyone was relieved that no one had stumbled upon that particular mushroom in the forest.

The day ended with grilled sausages and potatoes over the fire. Tuomas couldn't quite enjoy it. He had the uneasy feeling that Mirko and his friends were up to something.

Later, crawling into his bunk, a strange smell wafted up from his bedding. He lifted the corner of his pillow. There it was—an orange-red mushroom squashed between the mattress and his sleeping bag.

Of course.

Without a word, Tuomas turned the mattress over and went to sleep—but not before slipping the pungent mushroom into a paper towel and tucking it somewhere unexpected.

The next morning, Mirko appeared at breakfast, looking slightly uncomfortable and oddly quiet.

Perhaps it had something to do with the mushroom now residing in his own sleeping bag.

After breakfast, the class headed out in search of mosses and lichens.

They knew even less about mosses than mushrooms. To them, moss was just the soft green carpet between trees—a cushion for bare feet and forest creatures.

Ms. Puntanen gathered the group and began:

"Mosses are the superheroes of the plant world. They can survive on rocks, tree trunks, in water, on ice. They can handle drought, heat, frost—even radiation. Mosses conquered the earth over 450 million years ago, long before most other plants. There are over 250,000 species worldwide, and at least 884 right here in Finland. Scientists are even planning to take one type on space—to make medicine for astronauts."

That got their attention.

A few hours later, the students returned, some wet and muddy, but all proud of their samples. Väinö, always the lumbering one, had to be hauled out of a bog after sinking in knee-deep. He emerged triumphant, holding a clump of soggy peat moss like a prize.

Back at camp, the students gathered eagerly at their desks, and it didn't take long for Mirko to raise his hand.

"Hey Paula," he grinned, "are we hunting funny names again today?"

"You just want more ice cream," Ms. Puntanen said with a smile.

"No, the names are just too good!" he said, grinning.

Permission was granted.

"Wimpern-Krause!" someone shouted, pointing. "Elli, that's totally you!"

Laughter rang out as kids flipped through the books again. Lists filled with absurd plant names. One student muttered, "Who even comes up with these?"

Before the awards were handed out, Mirko raised another question. "Hey, is it like swearing or mocking when you call someone stuff like that?"

Ms. Puntanen paused thoughtfully. "Well... plant names aren't usually offensive. There are girls named Lily and Rose, after all."

That should have been the end of it.

But her answer unleashed something unexpected.

"In that case, Mia's mom is a clear birch hole sponge!" someone shouted.

Roars of laughter erupted. Soon the entire teaching staff had been assigned bizarre plant nicknames—ones that would resurface in whispers and giggles in the school hallways for weeks.

Ms. Puntanen eventually restored order—but not without resorting to her final weapon: confiscating the plant guides and promising math after lunch.

The class groaned.

Math and English, though less thrilling, helped settle the mood as the sun began to dip.

That evening, Grandpa Kuitunen appeared in the doorway, wiping his forehead with a rag.

"The sauna's ready!" he declared. "Hot as hell!"

The boys cheered. The camp was old-fashioned, and there were no showers in the main building. The kitchen boiler only supplied water for dishes. The sauna by the lake was the only option.

The girls opted to wait until the heat died down.

The boys, however, were eager to prove their bravery.

Mirko, naturally, had to comment. "Let's see what city leather can take," he said, eyeing Tuomas. Everyone knew he was from Helsinki.

Fortunately, no one knew that Tuomas barely had any sauna experience at all. His apartment in the city didn't have a private one, and his parents had never liked the shared one in the basement. Once, at the public pool, Tuomas had tried it with his dad, but the presence of sweaty strangers had driven him out in minutes.

In Sicily and Arkko, it had always been baths and showers.

Still, Tuomas said nothing. He pulled a towel from his backpack and followed the others into the sauna.

He could handle it. His skin was at least half Finnish.

Inside the wooden vestibule, the boys undressed without hesitation. Real Finns went to the sauna naked—only tourists wore swimsuits, which were unbearably uncomfortable when soaked with sweat.

Nudity wasn't the issue.

But the wooden slats under their bare bottoms?

Those were so hot the boys let out sharp gasps and awkward yelps as they sat, hopping slightly like frogs on a frying pan.

And so began Tuomas's first real test of fire.

All ten of them—Tuomas, Mirko, Matias, Huugo, Väinö, Onni, Toivo, Ville, Jesse, and Roope—sat side by side on the long wooden bench like chickens on a perch. Mirko, closest to the heater, had claimed the ladle and declared himself master of the infusion. And Grandpa Kuitunen hadn't been joking—he'd fired up the sauna like a furnace.

The very first ladle of water hit the stones with a sharp hiss, releasing a wave of steam so thick it wrapped around the boys like a blanket. Most of them ducked low, shielding their faces with their hands. All but Mirko and Tuomas.

Grinning mischievously, Mirko tossed a second ladle of water onto the stones.

More steam surged out.

The boys groaned, bent double in defense. Mirko cast a side glance at Tuomas, who was still sitting upright.

"I swear, this guy was born in a sauna and raised on a stove," he said, laughing at his own joke.

Another ladle. Someone coughed. Someone else groaned.

"You trying to boil us alive in here?"

"No devil could survive this!"

"Maniac!"

The first of them bolted for the door, racing into the cool anteroom and then across the beach to the lake. Their yelps echoed back as they plunged into the freezing water. Only five boys remained: Mirko, Tuomas, Huugo, Matias, and Väinö—who was so well insulated that the heat barely touched him.

"Only the weak fall by the wayside," Mirko quoted smugly and dumped another ladle onto the stones.

The temperature gauge ticked past 100°C. The wood creaked under the rising heat. Sweat rolled down their backs like streams.

Mirko leaned in closer, locking eyes with Tuomas.

"You don't have to prove anything," he said. "You can leave too, Väinö. This is between me and Tuomas."

That was enough for the others. Huugo, Matias, and even Väinö slipped out to the anteroom to watch through the wall.

Mirko shifted on the bench. "Still holding up, city boy?" he muttered.

Tuomas didn't flinch. "Feels great, actually."

And it wasn't a bluff. The sauna heat didn't bite or burn. It wrapped around him like a second skin—gentle, almost comforting. Even the steam in his lungs felt light and breathable, not scalding.

He didn't understand it, but he didn't question it either.

Mirko stared hard and dumped another ladle. Then another.

This time, the steam rose so violently that even Mirko flinched and leaned forward, gasping. But Tuomas didn't move. He leaned back casually, draping his arms across the bench's backrest.

"More space now," he said softly. "Much better."

Mirko glared at him. Then, in a sudden burst of frustration, he jumped up, grabbed the full bucket, and dumped the entire contents onto the stones in one go.

The stove hissed and cracked. A thunderous blast of steam erupted, filling every inch of the sauna.

But by the time the cloud settled, Mirko was already gone — slamming the door as he fled.

The boys in the anteroom stared at the closed door, frozen.

"He's still in there?" Jesse whispered.

"What if he passes out?" Toivo muttered. "We can't just leave him."

"If he dies, we're going to jail," Väinö added nervously.

"We're minors," Matias corrected. "They'd send us to reform school."

A few more agonizing minutes passed.

Then Mirko sprang to his feet. Without a word, he yanked the sauna door open. The others crowded behind him, breath held.

Tuomas sat alone on the bench, eyes closed, utterly calm.

When he heard the door creak, he opened his eyes slowly.

"You're welcome to join me," he said, his voice unbothered. "Plenty of heat for everyone. But I think I'll go for a swim now."

He rose, stretched, and walked past them without word.

The four boys stood in stunned silence, even Mirko rendered speechless.

Eventually, Mirko muttered, "Let's go to the lake too."

On their way down, they passed the others—Onni, Toivo, Ville, Jesse, and Roope—already returning from the water, wrapped in towels and shivering.

"Brrr… the lake felt like an ice hole!" Roope exclaimed.

"You wouldn't know an ice hole if you fell in one," Jesse said.

"I did fall in one once! While skating!"

"That's not the same," Ville scoffed. "Let's get back to the sauna before those two lunatics return."

Tuomas didn't stop to chat. He walked to the water's edge, dove in, and swam a lap with easy strokes. As he emerged, water streaming down his back, he caught movement out of the corner of his eye.

Four silhouettes stood on the pier, holding hands like they were about to jump together.

Then—SPLASH!

A single, massive splash followed.

Tuomas smiled faintly and headed back to the sauna to change.

"Who just ran to the pier?" one of the boys in the anteroom asked.

"Mirko, Matias, Huugo, and Väinö," Tuomas replied as he dried off.

"Väinö jumped too?" asked Onni, eyebrows raised.

Tuomas shrugged with a grin. "They all jumped. Väinö probably caused a tsunami."

Laughter exploded in the room.

The ice was broken. The challenge was over.

But Tuomas, they realed, was made of something diffe-rent.

Something not entirely explainable.

Something possibly not entirely… human.

"Väinö can't swim!"

The words hit Tuomas like a shockwave.

If the other boys had let go of him during the jump, Väi-nö might be drowning right now.

Tuomas didn't wait. He turned and sprinted down the narrow path to the beach, the others pounding after him in the dark.

Three naked, laughing figures appeared from the shadows—Mirko, Matias, and Huugo—dripping wet and catching their breath.

"Where's Väinö?" Tuomas shouted, his voice sharp with panic.

"He's coming," one of them said with a casual shrug. "Just a little slow—"

"He can't swim," Tuomas snapped. "Did you let go of his hand?"

There was a pause—then sudden dread in Matias's voice.

"The grip didn't hold... oh damn—Väinö!"

In a heartbeat, the whole group charged down to the dock.

The sky was overcast, the lake black as ink. Cold air stung their skin as they called out into the darkness.

"Väinö!"

"Väinö, can you hear us?!"

Nothing. No reply. No ripple. Only silence.

Tuomas scanned the water—nothing broke the surface. But he remembered where they had jumped and without a second thought, dove in.

A splash behind him—Mirko. Then another—Matias.

They dove down again and again, lungs burning, water pressing in. It was impossible to see anything, and even less to feel. Twice Mirko surfaced and collided with someone else.

"Väinö?"

"No—it's just me. Damn!"

Tuomas's chest ached. His ears rang. He was starting to lose hope.

And then—movement.

Two legs, kicking weakly beneath the dock. Then a pale blur.

Väinö.

He had latched desperately onto the metal ring that moored the summer boats, his fingers curled so tight they looked welded to the steel. His head bobbed just above the water, only his eyes and nostrils visible—like a frightened water rat.

Tuomas surfaced beside him. The moment his hand touched Väinö's back, the boy flinched and let go.

No!

Tuomas lunged, caught him, and hauled him back above water. Väinö sputtered, limbs flailing like a hooked fish. But Tuomas held on, guiding him through the water like a panicked, oversized toddler. Together, they made it to shore.

"He's here! Väinö's here!" Tuomas shouted, collapsing onto the sand beside him.

The others circled around, breathless and wide-eyed.

"Is he breathing?"

"Should we get Ms. Puntanen?"

"No way—we'll get in trouble!"

"Move!" Onni shoved his way forward and dropped to his knees. As part of the village's youth fire brigade, he knew what to do. He placed his hands on Väinö's chest and started rhythmic compressions.

Tuomas knelt beside them, still catching his breath.

Just as Onni leaned in to begin mouth-to-mouth, Väinö stirred.

"You... you don't have to hug me," he mumbled, eyes fluttering open.

Laughter broke out around the group, nervous but relieved.

Väinö coughed, sat up, and looked around. "I think," he said, "it's really time I learn how to swim."

"How did you even make it back to the dock?".

"I think Tuomas—" Väinö stopped.

He remembered something.

Not Tuomas.

Something else.

Two glowing red eyes under the dock. Just for a moment. Watching him.

A chill ran through him. And it wasn't from the cold.

When they were finally dressed again, Mirko turned to the group and said quietly, "We don't talk about this."

Everyone nodded.

When they returned to the camp, the teachers were surprised by how unusually quiet the boys were. No one cracked jokes. No one teased. Just polite nods and zipped lips.

Later, lying in bed, Tuomas stared at the dark ceiling.

Are you even human? Mirko had asked.

Of course he was. He was tired, hungry, and needed to pee. All very human things.

But then again... wasn't Jesus also human—and something else? God and man? Was that even possible?

Tuomas didn't have an answer. But the question sed to leave him.

If he wasn't just human...

...then what was he?

31

Rain had poured down during the night, drenching the forest floor. The morning air was cool and damp, heavy with the scent of wet moss and pine. With the ground still soaked and the trails slippery, Ms. Puntanen called off the morning's outdoor activities and ordered regular lessons instead.

After lunch, the schedule would lighten up. Grandpa Kuitunen, a lifelong fisherman, was slated to give a talk about Finnish fish—and if the weather allowed, maybe even take the students out for a little fishing.

The students, however, were far more curious about the evening's "surprise program."

But then came an unexpected hitch.

Miranda's mother had to leave. Her elderly neighbor—who was supposed to feed the chickens—had slipped and possibly broken something. Anneli Mattila didn't quite trust the woman on her own and felt she had no choice but to drive her to the hospital. Fortunately, she'd brought her own car for exactly this sort of emergency.

After dinner, Ms. Puntanen finally revealed the secret:

"Tonight, we're going on a night hike."

A ripple of excitement spread through the room.

"We'll head out in three groups, each led by an adult. We'll walk at least a kilometer into the forest and sit quietly to observe nature at night. No phones, no talking—just listen. What moves in the darkness? What sounds do you hear when humans fall silent?"

She paused, then added, "Only the group leaders may carry flashlights. We'll switch them off when we reach our destination. Tomorrow morning, you'll each write about what you experienced."

A nervous voice piped up from the back. "But... this peninsula is called Susiniemi. That means Wolf Island. What if there are wolves?"

"There are no wolves here," Mia's mother said calmly. "And even if there were, they're far more afraid of you than you are of them."

The kids played board games while dusk fell. Black clouds rolled back in. The air turned thick and uneasy.

"I hope that storm doesn't come back," muttered Grandpa Kuitunen, who had just been promoted from firewood manager to group leader.

"Not in September," Ms. Puntanen said optimistically.

By nightfall, all three groups had disappeared into the forest.

Within thirty minutes, each group had spread out, far from camp and each other. They found spots beneath the trees and settled in. Some sat cross-legged, others lay flat on the forest floor, all listening—hearts thumping, breath held—for the mysterious sounds of night.

Just as the forest quieted, a flash lit up the sky. Then another. And another.

A cold wind swept through the aspen trees, turning leaves into a trembling chorus. Thunder rumbled low across the sky. Then came the first raindrops—fat, heavy, and cold.

The adults recognized the danger instantly. A storm in the forest—especially a violent one—could be deadly. In moments, a full-blown squall was raging.

"Back to camp!" came the shouted orders from all directions.

The children ran, disoriented and soaked, tripping over roots and rocks. The flashlight beams waved wildly, cutting through the dark like panicked signals. Shouting, crying, and curses echoed through the trees.

Slowly, the scattered groups reassembled around their leaders, huddled in the rain. Lightning sliced the sky. Thunder growled above. Somewhere in the darkness, a tree cracked and crashed to the forest floor.

No one had raincoats. Most were in T-shirts and shorts. They were soaked to the bone.

How are we going to dry them all before tomorrow? Ms. Puntanen worried. They'll all be sick...

At last, the lights of the camp shimmered through the trees—golden halos in the gloom. Shouting, laughing, and groaning, the students burst from the forest and ran for the safety of the main building.

In the great hall, the teacher immediately began roll call, ticking off names with trembling fingers.

Then Mia's voice cut through the room.

"Where's Miranda?"

Silence.

Ms. Puntanen scanned the soggy group of students—no sign of Miranda's golden curls.

"You left her in the woods?" Her voice cracked.

"She was with us when the lightning hit," said one of the girls in Grandpa Kuitunen's group. "We all got up and ran. It was chaos. No one thought to take her hand..."

As if summoned by fate, the next bolt of lightning struck —followed by a loud pop—and the entire building went black.

"It's okay," Grandpa Kuitunen said, trying to stay calm. "The generator should kick in any second."

But a minute passed.

Then two.

Still nothing.

"I don't think we have a generator," Ms. Puntanen whispered.

"I'll check the fuse box," Grandpa Kuitunen said, grabbing a flashlight. But the box was fine. No blown fuse. Just darkness.

They scrambled for candles. Within minutes, small flames flickered in mugs and dishes on the long dining table, casting ghostly shadows on the walls.

"We have to find Miranda!" Ms. Puntanen said urgently. "She's alone out there—in this storm."

She was already picturing the conversation she'd have to have with Anneli Mattila. We lost your blind daughter in a thunderstorm...

Even if Miranda had been assigned to Grandpa Kuitunen's group, the responsibility fell on the teacher. It always did.

"Girls," she said, "you have to show us where you last saw her."

"I'm not going back out there!" one of them cried, close to tears. "I don't even know where we were! We just followed Grandpa Kuitunen—I didn't look where we were going!"

"Then you will have to lead the way," Ms. Puntanen said, turning to the old man.

Grandpa Kuitunen nodded grimly.

Outside, the storm raged on.

But somewhere in that black forest, Miranda was waiting.

But Kai's grandfather didn't move.

He sank heavily onto the bench, clutching his chest with both hands, his breath ragged and shallow.

"It hurts," he gasped. "My chest… my heart again…"

A heavy silence fell.

Not now.

In the middle of a thunderstorm, in a powerless building deep in the woods, with the most vulnerable student missing—now their only male chaperone was possibly having a heart attack.

Ms. Puntanen stiffened, then pulled her phone from her pocket and dialed the emergency number. It took a moment to connect. The storm had likely knocked out half the region's lines. Finally, someone answered.

She gave the details as calmly as she could, voice clipped, professional. A heart patient in distress. A child lost in the woods. No electricity. No generator. A storm overhead.

When she hung up, she turned away from the others for a moment and exhaled deeply, gathering herself.

"Help is on the way," she said. "But the power company says fallen trees and damaged lines mean we'll be thout electricity for the time being."

A boy raised his hand hesitantly. "What if… what if a helicopter came?"

"Yeah, in those rescue movies they always send a copter," someone added.

Paula shook her head.

"No helicopter will fly in this storm. And even if they could, they wouldn't land here—it's too dark, too dangerous. The nearest chopper is based in Kuopio. That's 150 kilometers away. We're on our own for now."

Kai suddenly burst into tears. "But what if Grandpa dies?!"

"And Miranda?" another voice cried. "What if she gets struck by lightning—or if wolves find her?!"

The girls were spiraling into panic now, voices rising, faces pale. Ms. Puntanen felt it too—that cold wave of fear rising inside her, threatening to drown her. But she bit it down. She had been in the army. She had passed her first aid certifications. She was the adult.

She turned to the old man, who lay hunched on the bench, his breathing shallow.

"Can you tell me roughly where your group went?" she asked gently.

"We headed toward the tip of the peninsula," he murmured. "There's… a path."

Paula turned to Mia's mother. "You stay here. You're the only adult now. Look after the students and keep Kuitunen warm. Give him water if he can drink. Tell the kids to get into dry clothes—whatever they can find in the dark— and crawl into their sleeping bags to warm up."

Then she grabbed a flashlight and headed for the door.

But no one noticed that Tuomas had already slipped out —long before anyone had mentioned the search.

He had joined Grandpa Kuitunen's group on purpose. He was worried about Miranda. He knew she'd have trouble navigating the woods on her own. But during the hike, the other girls had taken such good care of her, he'd assumed all was well.

He hadn't realized they'd left her behind in the confusion.

Now, as the panic spread through the camp, Tuomas was already racing through the forest, alone.

But he wasn't afraid.

He didn't need a flashlight. The path unfolded before him, sharp and clear. Stones, roots, branches—he saw everything. Even in pitch darkness, the forest wasn't dark for him. His eyes had adjusted without him noticing.

He didn't understand why the others were so helpless at night.

He ran faster, almost gliding through the trees. His feet barely touched the ground. He was past the wet under-growth, past the crooked birch trees, past the fallen log someone had stumbled over earlier.

He reached the hollow where they had waited for the forest to speak.

But it was empty now.

No sign of Miranda.

His chest tightened.

Had she panicked and run deeper into the forest? Maybe toward the beach? What if she'd fallen? What if she was lying unconscious in a ditch—or worse—what if the lake had swallowed her in the storm?

He stood perfectly still, eyes scanning the shadows, ears straining against the wind.

Then he stepped forward, deeper into the dark.

He would find her.

He had to.

"Miranda!" Tuomas shouted into the trees. "MIRANDA!"

His voice echoed through the storm-drenched forest, swallowed by wind and rain.

Then—a flicker of movement beneath a low fir tree.

He ran closer.

Miranda.

She was curled beneath the branches, soaked and shivering, her arms wrapped tightly around her knees.

Far behind them, Paula Puntanen trudged through the forest alone, tears streaming down her face and mixing with the rain. She had held it together for hours—for the children, for Kuitunen, for the other adults—but now, in the storm-lit solitude, despair broke through.

A missing child. A heart patient. No electricity. No backup. And no guarantee anyone would make it through the night unscathed.

It felt like failure.

Her flashlight flickered across the slippery path. She pushed forward, sobbing silently, searching for any sign of the lost girl.

She stepped into a clearing just as lightning split the sky.

And there—on the far side—stood a dark, massive figure.

A bear? An elk?

Her breath caught. Her heart slammed against her ribs.

Then a second bolt of lightning lit up the clearing—and for a split second, the creature shimmered with a glowing dome of light before it collapsed to the ground in a burst of sparks.

Back beneath the fir, Tuomas struggled to pull Miranda to her feet. She was stiff with fear and nearly unresponsive.

"Come on," he whispered. "It's okay now. You're safe."

But she wouldn't move.

She was older. Heavier. He couldn't carry her—not like this.

If only I were strong enough, Tuomas thought. Like King Kong, carrying that girl in the old movie.

And then—something impossible happened.

A shadow emerged from the forest. Massive. Gentle.

It knelt beside them, lifted Miranda into its arms, and leapt back toward camp with uncanny grace.

At the forest's edge, just as Paula arrived with her flashlight, the creature lowered Miranda gently to the ground —right before lightning struck again.

The bolt hit the figure directly.

Its arms curled protectively over Miranda, channeling the lightning's deadly force through its own body and into the roots of an old pine. The trunk hissed, then blackened. The creature vanished.

Only Tuomas remained, standing calmly beside the stunned girl.

"Hi, Paula," he said, as if nothing unusual had happened. "Miranda's here. She's just a little wet."

"Miranda!" Paula rushed forward, dropping to her knees and pulling the girl into her arms.

"Oh, my poor child—are you all right?"

"I'm okay," Miranda whispered. "Tuomas found me."

Paula didn't let go of her hand until they were safely back at the camp.

When they stepped through the door, the others broke into relieved cheers. Tuomas was briefly enveloped in praise and hugs, though Paula silently wondered how he had managed to find Miranda so quickly—and whether what she had seen in the clearing had been real or a figment of storm-fueled fear.

Meanwhile, Mia's mother answered a call from the emergency room. The doctor gave instructions for keeping Grandpa Kuitunen stable. Paramedics would arrive at first light—lumber crews were already being dispatched to clear the storm-felled trees blocking the road.

Kuitunen lay wrapped in blankets, warm and calm. The pain had subsided.

"I'm sorry for the fuss," he said. "Forgot my nitroglycerin tablets. Rookie mistake."

The students had changed into dry clothes by flashlight and candlelight. The storm had stolen their sleep, but once Tuomas and Miranda returned, exhaustion finally settled over the room. Wet clothes were draped over chairs and benches. No one had the energy to move them.

Just before dawn, the distant roar of chainsaws echoed through the forest.

A knock at the door.

Two paramedics entered with a stretcher. They gently checked Kuitunen's pulse and blood pressure, then carried him out to the waiting ambulance.

By breakfast, the forest road was passable. The students packed their bags.

Camp was over.

"You've had enough nature for one lifetime," the director joked weakly.

Miranda's mother arrived not long after, furious at first.

"How could you let this happen? You left her alone in the woods—blind!"

But after seeing Miranda safe and hearing her version of the story, her anger softened. She accepted the teacher's apology—and offered Tuomas a tearful hug.

"She says you were the one who saved her," she said quietly.

Tuomas didn't know how to respond. He just nodded.

That night, back home, he stood in the bathroom and looked at himself in the mirror.

Just a skinny boy stared back.

No King Kong. No glowing giant.

Overactive imagination, he thought.

And yet… there was something in his eyes.

Something not quite explainable.

The following week, during recess, Mirko approached Tuomas. Alone.

He glanced around to make sure no one was nearby, then cleared his throat.

Tuomas braced for another insult.

Instead, Mirko said, "Hey. I just wanted to say—I'm sorry. I was a jerk at camp. You were right. You didn't deserve that."

Tuomas blinked. "Forget it."

Mirko hesitated. "I guess… I was jealous. You have this cool house. And your dad… My dad was just a factory worker. He drowned in a snowmobile accident when my little sister was a baby."

Tuomas's expression softened. "Was his name Reijo? I've heard of him. My dad said they used to be friends."

"Yeah," Mirko said, surprised. "That was him."

"I'm sorry. And… I don't see my dad that often either. And that house? It's not as great as it looks."

Mirko nodded. "Yeah. Still."

He turned and walked away.

Not a friendship.

But maybe, just maybe—a truce.

32

During the Christmas holidays, Tuomas's father kept his promise. He took the week before Christmas off and booked a trip for just the two of them—destination: Munich. There would be no gloomy Arvola streets with a single blinking tree outside the local store. Instead, there would be glowing lights, music, steaming mulled wine, and gifts from around the world.

"We'll find something nice for Alma and Grandma," his father said. "And we'll visit the Bavaria Film Studios—see where The NeverEnding Story and those submarine movies were filmed."

Tuomas had lit up at the very idea. A trip with his father, a real city adventure, and a flight—nothing about that could compare to staying in damp, quiet Arvola, where even the ice rink hadn't opened yet thanks to an unusually warm December.

The airport had been the first thrill. Tuomas stood proudly as his father introduced him to colleagues with a hand on his shoulder: "This is my son, Tuomas." It made him feel older, seen.

Their first morning in Munich, after a hotel breakfast of croissants and hot chocolate, they set off for the famed Christmas market. The Marienplatz greeted them with a 30-meter Christmas tree gleaming with thousands of lights. The square pulsed with festive music, and the scent of roasted almonds and cinnamon filled the air.

Both sides of the pedestrian street were lined with rows of decorated stalls—hundreds of them. Candles, glass ornaments, wooden toys, gingerbread hearts, woolen scarves, and music boxes. The crowd flowed like a living river: tourists snapping photos, families holding hands, couples with steaming mugs in mittened hands.

Tuomas soaked it all in. He bought a snow globe for Alma—an alpine cabin nestled in powdered flakes that danced every time he shook it. Now, he was browsing postcards for Grandma. She loved real cards, even in this digital age. She'd display it proudly on her dresser.

His father had wandered off to wait in a long line for the restroom after one too many mugs of mulled wine.

That's when it happened.

Tuomas felt a searing heat beneath his shirt. He flinched. The Nonna stone—his grandmother's gift—was burning against his chest.

What are you trying to tell me, Nonna? he asked silently, alarmed.

And then came the sound—first shrill whistles, then shouting, then screaming.

A wave of tension rippled through the market.

People turned. Heads rose. Some began moving nervously away from the main street.

Tuomas, shorter than most, saw only the growing unease—until he caught a glimpse of movement between the stalls. In the distance, something massive.

A truck.

Speeding straight into the pedestrian zone.

No. No. It's one of those terror attacks. Like in the news.

The crowd began to scatter. Screams rose. People shoved and scrambled behind stalls and barriers, knocking over displays as they fled.

Tuomas wanted to run too—but then he saw him.

A man in a wheelchair, frozen in place in the middle of the road. Confused. Paralyzed by panic.

No one stopped. No one helped. Everyone was running.

Tuomas didn't think. He couldn't.

Images flashed through his mind: the beach in Arvola. Mirko's taunt. The moment he had turned into a stone pillar to protect himself.

But now—this wasn't about him. This required something bigger.

In his mind, he saw the Arkko farm stables—centuries-old granite walls, unmoving and eternal.

He imagined them rising, forming not a barrier, but a fortress.

At the wheel of the truck, the driver—a man drugged beyond fear, driven only by violent purpose—saw only a blur: a boy beside a motionless man in a wheelchair.

They weren't moving.

They weren't afraid.

Then the world shattered.

There was a deafening crash, the sound of metal folding into itself. The truck didn't swerve or slow—it hit something it couldn't see.

The front crumpled like paper. Steel screeched. Glass exploded outward. The cab compacted with brutal force.

And then, silence.

A stunned, eerie hush.

Until the screaming resumed.

People rushed forward—cautious, shaken—toward the wreck.

The truck's hood was smashed into the engine block. Its cab twisted in on itself like an accordion. Later, firemen would have to weld the driver's remains out of the wreckage.

But Tuomas stood still. His heart still pounding. The stone now cool against his skin.

No one had seen him move. No one had seen what had really stopped the truck.

His father came running through the crowd, eyes wide with panic, scanning for his son.

"Tuomas!" he shouted. "Are you all right? What happened?"

"I'm okay," Tuomas said, though his voice trembled.

All around them, chaos reigned.

But Tuomas felt something different.

A strange stillness inside himself.

A new line had been crossed.

The first police officer to reach the scene had been stationed at the roadblock. He'd seen the truck plow past and, knowing he couldn't stop it, had sprinted after it anyway—submachine gun drawn, ready to fire if the vehicle halted.

But the truck hadn't stopped.

When he arrived at the crash site, he aimed his weapon at the twisted wreckage. More officers and emergency responders quickly closed in, pushing back the crowd. There was still a possibility the truck was wired to explode.

Instead, they found three more terrorists crumpled in the cargo hold. The impact had flung them around like rag dolls, and their weapons lay scattered and useless. The attack had failed—but not without cost.

Several lives had been lost under the wheels of the truck. Dozens were injured. Blood stained the cobblestones where festive lights still flickered.

Tuomas, unnoticed in the chaos, had pushed the wheelchair user to safety and left him near a booth. The man sat slumped, his head tilted, his limbs motionless. He hardly understood what had happened, and he couldn't explain anything when the police came. His condition was so advanced he could neither speak nor write.

Later, in the days leading up to Christmas, the story made headlines across Europe. Many called it a miracle. Eyewitnesses swore they had seen holy figures—the Virgin Mary, even the baby Jesus—emerging from the light to protect the crowd.

At the Church of the Holy Spirit, an impromptu service was held. They sang hymns through tears and praised God for sending an angel. The donation box overflowed again and again.

But journalists weren't done.

They tracked down every detail of the man in the wheelchair's life. Though he'd done nothing—nothing but be there, alive—he was hailed as a savior. When the public discovered he lived in a crumbling apartment with his elderly mother, donations poured in. A better home was arranged. A brighter life promised.

But he wouldn't live to see it.

One year later, he succumbed to his illness. His mother quietly vanished into the folds of the social care system. The apartment was locked, emptied, forgotten.

Tuomas knew none of this when he left the man by the booth and went looking for his father.

His father had only just learned about the attack—he'd been in the restroom during the chaos. Now he saw his son pale and visibly shaken, and didn't press for details. Tuomas asked to go back to the hotel immediately.

On the way, his father said casually, "Where's your hat? Put it on—it's winter."

"Uh… I guess I lost it in the crowd," Tuomas said quickly.

In truth, he had placed it gently on the man's head. The poor guy had been sitting for hours, cold and bareheaded. The cap—blue, with white stars—was distinctive. Tuomas had a sudden, anxious thought: the security cameras must have picked it up. But now it was on someone else.

In the confusion, no one had noticed that earlier it had covered a red-haired boy's curls.

Back in the hotel, the TV blared with breaking news. Footage played over and over—an aerial shot of the truck's final stretch through the Christmas market. Screams. Blurs. People diving for cover. Then—

A flash.

The image glitched.

It became overexposed, then blurry—right where the truck should have struck.

When the feed resumed, police had surrounded the wreck. Cameras refocused. But that moment—that critical moment—was lost.

Tuomas let out a slow, shaking breath. No sign of him. No one had seen.

His father, oblivious to the storm raging inside him, offered dinner at the hotel restaurant. But Tuomas declined.

"You should rest," his father said gently. "You've… been through a lot. After what happened. I know it must remind you of the car accident. Your mother. Your uncle. It's okay to feel shaken."

Tuomas nodded silently.

When his father left the room, Tuomas lay on the bed. Not to sleep.

To think.

To fear.

He had killed a man.

The news confirmed it—the truck driver had died instantly. Tuomas remembered his face. The wild stare behind the windshield. That split second before impact.

And then it happened again.

That was what terrified him most. Not the crash. Not the death. But the force that had emerged from inside him. Unseen. Uncontrolled.

What am I?

He remembered what Mirko had shouted in the sauna, weeks ago:

"Are you even human?"

Tuomas didn't know anymore.

Was he human… or something else?

A tool of good—or of something darker?

He desperately wanted to tell someone. Anyone. But who could he trust?

His father? Alma? Grandma?

No. They'd be horrified. Maybe even afraid of him. Maybe they'd lock him away—put him in a psychiatric hospital.

So Tuomas did the only thing he could.

He whispered a vow into the stillness of the hotel room:

"Never again. No more miracles. No more heroics. No more…"

His eyes burned with unshed tears.

"No more monster."

33

Tuomas was unusually quiet for the rest of the vacation in Munich. So quiet, in fact, that his father began to worry. He called home to reassure Grandma and Alma that everything was fine. But before they returned, he gave them a gentle warning: Don't ask Tuomas any questions about the attack. He's traumatized. Let him forget it, if he can.

After landing in Helsinki, Tuomas made a surprising request: he wanted to visit his old hometown.

Olli Arkko had recently bought a furnished three-room apartment in North Haaga from a fellow pilot relocating to Dubai. The price had been fair for a flat in an aging complex, and the furniture was modest—perfect for a man who didn't need much.

But when Olli brought his young Italian wife there, she'd added her own touches: Persian rugs, porcelain angels, ballet figurines, and oversized plastic flower arrangements that leaned awkwardly from every vase.

As the elevator rattled upward, Tuomas felt a strange sense of déjà vu. The nameplates on the apartment doors had hardly changed. Mrs. Pietarinen—who used to scold him for his muddy boots—still lived next door. The Laaksos' mailbox hung slightly open, and their dog's nose poked out curiously. A pile of yellowing flyers and unpaid bills lay scattered on the floor. Tuomas stepped over them and stared down the stairwell from the fifth floor.

He hadn't looked at the world from such a height in a long time. Since moving to Arvola, his window view had been nothing but apple trees and a lonely windmill.

But what hurt most was what wasn't there.

The absence of his mother.

Every room whispered of her. Dried plants hung sadly in pots that had once overflowed with her vibrant flowers. Her favorite scarf lay on the armchair—still loosely folded, as if she'd just stepped out. Her slippers peeked out from beneath the chair, forgotten.

Tuomas felt something in him crack.

"I hardly came here," he whispered. "The flowers died too… Everything feels so empty."

He walked slowly through the rooms, half-hoping to find her, half-dreading it. When he reached the bookshelf, he found photos among the porcelain. A wedding portrait. His mother as a flight attendant. A photo of her holding newborn Tuomas, her smile brighter than any memory.

He ran his fingers over the frame.

And then—he heard it.

A whisper.

"Tuomas… Tommaso mio…"

He spun around, heart pounding. No one was there. The room was silent.

But the voice continued—in his mind, not in his ears.

"Sono sempre con te. Prenditi cura di tuo padre. Ti amo..."

I am always with you. Take care of your father. I love you.

And just like that, the voice faded.

Tuomas's chest ached with the intensity of it. She had to exist somewhere.

Just then, Olli entered the room and saw Tuomas holding the photo.

"You can take it with you," his father said gently. "If it doesn't make you too sad. The past… it's gone. We can't bring it back, no matter how hard we wish."

"She's not completely gone," Tuomas said quietly.

"Sure. She lives in our memories. Still, I wish she hadn't been buried in Italy. We can't even bring her flowers."

"She's with her family in Marradi."

"You speak so wisely." Olli smiled faintly. "I'm lucky to have you."

Tuomas began gathering the things he wanted to take: old photo albums, a few games, clothes that still smelled faintly of her. He packed one of her large, fluffy feather pillows into a plastic bag. It still held the soft scent of her hair.

"Do you think I'll ever live here again?" he asked.

"Maybe when you're older. If you study in Helsinki—or if I ever stop flying and stay home more."

So… maybe never.

Olli Arkko would fly until retirement, and Tuomas wasn't even sure if he wanted to go to university.

They returned to the Arkko estate that same evening.

Later that night, Jaska visited Tuomas in his room. The strange spirit had a way of knowing when he was needed.

Tuomas let the words spill out.

"What's happening to me, Jaska? What am I? A human can't do what I did. If I'm not human… then what?"

Jaska scratched his head. "You're not an elf. Not a goblin. Not even a church ghost." Looked unsettled. "Strange, really strange…"

That night, Tuomas took the photo of his mother to bed with him. Under the soft light of his bedside lamp, he stroked the image, trying to lock in every detail—her smile, her voice, her way of pronouncing his name in Italian:

"Tommaso, caro Tommaso… angelo mio."

He whispered, "Mama… Mama… What am I? I'm scared."

A breeze seemed to pass through the room.

And then he heard the whisper again—faint and, like his mother used to speak: part Italian, part English, part dream.

"Non avere paura… Nonna ha un segreto… Secret… don't tell… Ask Nonna…"

Nonna has a secret…

Tuomas's mother had always mixed languages, sometimes leading to confusion—but this was different. This felt like a clue. A message.

He thought of Nonna, his Italian grandmother. Her light blue eyes—like his. His mother had brown eyes, dark hair. But Tuomas? Flaming red hair. Wild and untamed.

"Where did I get this from?" he wondered. Nonna had always worn a black headscarf. He'd never seen what lay beneath it.

He grabbed one of the old photo albums and flipped through it. Strangely, there were no wedding pictures of his grandparents. Not a single one.

Tomorrow, he thought. I'll ask Chiara. Maybe Nonna told her the secret. Whatever it is.

Life on the Arkko estate slowly became bearable.

Alma made sure of that. She introduced Tuomas to the house's long history and the faces on the walls: officers, clergymen, politicians, and businessmen.

"Quite a family tree," Tuomas murmured.

One afternoon, Alma drove him through the village.

"There used to be a bakery here," she said. "A general store over there. Even a little movie theater and police station. You should've seen the crowd at the train station…"

155

Tuomas interrupted. "You always talk about what used to be here. But now there's nothing. What happened? Did aliens invade? Where did it all go?"

Alma sighed. "The world's changing, Tuomas. Even in Arvola. People drive into the city now. The stores closed. The services faded. TV actors are more familiar than your own neighbors. People don't even greet each other on the street anymore."

She looked at him wistfully.

"What will it be like," she said, "when you're my age?"

34

By the time winter settled fully over Arvola, Tuomas had found his rhythm. School had become routine. The ice rink was the village's heartbeat, and Tuomas was now fully accepted among the hockey-playing boys. It felt good—normal—to belong. He rarely thought about his strange powers anymore. Maybe it had all just been a phase.

The rink itself was modest—just a frozen patch maintained by volunteers—but for the youth of Arvola, it was more than enough. For the boys from nearby Birkendorf, however, it held a different kind of draw. Although technically a city district, Birkendorf lay on the outskirts, closer to farmland than to skyscrapers. When they skated in the city, the locals mocked them.

"Yokels on the road again! What's that smell—cow dung?"

Humiliated and bitter, the boys from Birkendorf began showing up at the Arvola rink, determined to prove they weren't to be messed with.

On a snowy Sunday afternoon, Tuomas was playing hockey with a group of friends when he noticed trouble brewing.

Kai Kuitunen had come with his older sister, Maija. Their parents had dropped them off, promising to return later with pizza. Maija, who had Down syndrome and only came home from her care facility on weekends, stood alone on the ice while her younger brother joined the game.

"You got this, Maija! Go skate!" Kai had called before vanishing into the crowd.

Maija could skate well enough, but all the bustling people made her nervous. She hovered near the boards, smiling shyly in the way that was typical for her—gentle, unthreatening, open-hearted.

At the far end of the rink, Tuomas had been watching a group of four tall boys—the unmistakable Birkendorf crew. They'd been goofing off, pulling stunts, deliberately bumping into younger kids. They had that restless, aggressive energy that signaled they were looking for trouble.

Now, they were skating toward Maija.

Tuomas narrowed his eyes.

One of the boys—tall, blond, full of himself—glided right up to her and leaned in, grinning.

"What's this pretty girl doing all alone?" he cooed. "Were you waiting for me?"

Maija, flustered, smiled wider. She didn't understand the danger. She never did.

The boy reached out and gently lifted her chin.

"May I kiss the young lady?"

He leaned in.

Maija glanced around in confusion, searching for her brother, for anyone.

The other boys circled closer, snickering.

Tuomas was already on his way.

His skates cut across the ice like blades.

No more miracles. No more heroics, he had once promised.

But not today.

Just as the boy moved in to kiss Maija, something strange happened.

He suddenly spun—abruptly, inexplicably—and grabbed one of his friends instead. Then, without hesitation, he kissed him. Hard. Their noses knocked together with a crunch.

The two boys looked stunned—but the kiss didn't stop.

It deepened.

The other two backed away, horrified.

"Dude! Cut it out! People are watching!" one of them yelled, his voice cracking.

A crowd had started to gather. Matias, ever ready, already had his phone out.

"This is gold!" he cried. "The passionate Birkendorf boys on ice!"

One of the stunned teens lunged toward him. "Drop the phone, you little freak!"

He swung—missed—and slipped on the ice, crashing straight into the tangled, kissing duo. The fourth boy tried to escape but wiped out too, skidding helplessly across the rink.

Meanwhile, Maija was safely back on the opposite side, blinking in confusion.

Tuomas stood calmly between her and the chaos, arms folded.

"If you harass anyone here again," he said flatly, "this video goes online. Let's see who's laughing then."

The Birkendorf boys disentangled themselves and scrambled to their feet, faces red with shock, rage, and something else—humiliation.

"What the hell did you do to me?" one of them growled, wiping his mouth with the back of his glove.

"You kissed me, dude," the other muttered. Then, after a pause, added with a shrug, "To be honest… it wasn't that bad."

The third boy slapped the back of his head. "Shut up."

The group skated off, heads down, mumbling curses, and disappeared toward their car.

"Idiots," Matias muttered, stopping the recording. "But man, this video turned out great."

Tuomas didn't respond.

He just watched the horizon, snow falling softly around him, wondering how much longer he could keep pretending not to be what he was.

35

That spring, Tuomas received a troubling email from Chiara: Nonna Olivia says she's going to die soon. She wants to see you before it happens. This morning, she made pasta for the freezer and said it was for her funeral. Mom laughed—Nonna's never been sick a day in her life—but she seemed serious. So I'm writing you.

Nonna Olivia had always been thin as a broomstick and, by all guesses, at least ninety. No one had ever seen her birth certificate. Still, it was hard to imagine her dying. But Tuomas' father, Olli, agreed he should go. Tuomas and Nonna had always shared a special bond. Now that Tuomas was finally healthy again, there was no reason to stay behind. The school granted him a week off for "family reasons," and Olli took a few days off too.

They flew to Florence and rented a car to reach their relatives. By evening, they were winding up the hill toward Ristorante La Colombaia in the small town of Marradi. When Tuomas stepped out of the car, he was met by the soft chirring of crickets—so loud, it was like being dropped into a living symphony. It had still been cold in Finland, but here the air smelled of sun-warmed hay and the climbing roses that twined around the stone pillars on the terrace. In the garden, old Bruno barked from his chain, more out of habit than malice.

All the lights in the upstairs windows were blazing. As usual for a Saturday, the restaurant was packed. The main parking lot and even the driveway were full, but Olli navigated smoothly to a space around back. They entered through the side door and went straight into the heat and clatter of the kitchen.

Sofia stood over a large skillet, flipping sizzling steaks, her brow damp with sweat. Waitresses darted in and out with arms full of plates, the kitchen a flurry of controlled chaos.

"Grandma's resting in her room," Sofia said, barely looking up. "Chiara's still doing homework, but she'll come down for dinner. Nonna knows you're here—she specifically asked for Tommaso to go to her room as soon as he arrives. I don't know what she wants to tell him."

There was an edge in Sofia's voice. She clearly didn't like being excluded, especially from something so serious. Not even Chiara was allowed to hear.

"You go ahead," Olli said, inhaling deeply. "I'll eat first. With smells like these, who could resist?"

Tuomas grabbed his backpack and climbed the narrow, creaking staircase. At the top, he paused at Nonna's door, knocked softly, and pushed it open.

A dim bedside lamp cast a pool of golden light across the room. Nonna was sitting up with effort, her thin frame nearly swallowed by the pillows and her nightgown. Tuomas blinked—had she always been this small? Or had he grown that much since winter?

"Mio caro Tommaso! Bello mio!" she cried, opening her arms.

He rushed into them, folding into her frail embrace. Her chest barely rose under the thin fabric, and he felt her tears on his cheek.

"You came," she whispered, holding his face in her hands. "I didn't want to die before I could see you again. Before I could tell you."

"Oh, Nonna, don't talk like that," Tuomas whispered. "You're not going to die."

"But I know when my time has come," she said quietly. "There's so much you need to hear. Secrets that only you must know. Not Chiara. Not Sofia. Not even your father. I didn't tell your mother or Uncle Carlo—because it wasn't necessary. I thank Fate that they were allowed to die the right death."

The right death? Tuomas frowned, searching her face. Was she delirious? Her voice was clear, but her words made no sense.

Nonna leaned back into the pillows. For the first time in his memory, she wasn't wearing her black headscarf. Her red hair—nearly the same deep, fiery shade as his—fanned out across the pillow like a lion's mane.

"You know, Tommaso," she began, her voice more serious now, "I didn't want children. Not at first. I was already old when your mother was born. And then Carlo. I lived in fear that my children would be punished for what I had done—for my disobedience. That my people would come for them. The people of the volcano."

She paused. Tuomas stared.

"That's why we came here," she continued. "Far from Sicily. Your grandfather and I built a new life. The children were born here, and I thought we were safe. I thought it was over."

Her eyes searched his face, and something in her gaze sent a chill through him.

"But then you were born. And when I saw the first photo of you—your eyes, your hair—I knew. The legacy lives on in you. The legacy of the Lava People. Maybe the bloodline grew even stronger in the north. Perhaps your Finnish side carries old magic too. Wizards. Witches. Spirits. Who knows what powers sleep in your father's family?"

Tuomas opened his mouth, but no words came. What was she saying? Volcano people? Magic? But something in the way she spoke—the gravity of it—kept him silent. The clatter of dishes, Sofia's sharp commands, the laughter from the restaurant below—they all faded into a background hum. The world outside the room disappeared.

There was only Nonna. And the ancient secret she was about to pass on.

"Tommaso, everything I'm about to tell you is true. And it's my duty to tell you."

Nonna's voice trembled, but not from weakness—there was purpose behind it. Her gaze locked with Tuomas'.

"You have a little laptop, don't you? All kids have one now, even Chiara."

"I have a tablet in my backpack," Tuomas replied.

"Good. Take it out and record everything I say. You won't understand it all yet—and you won't remember it all either. But one day, you'll need to listen again."

Tuomas pulled the tablet from his bag, set it on the edge of the nightstand, and activated the voice recorder. Nonna let out a sigh of relief, closed her eyes briefly, and then began.

"Tommaso… there are beings in this world—life forms —that people know nothing about. Look at me: I was not always human. I once belonged to the Lava People."

Tuomas blinked. "The lava people? What… what is that?"

"The Lava People came into being long before humans. In the beginning, Earth wasn't solid—it was a swirling mass of gas and fire. Over millions of years, life experimented with many forms. Some were visible—plants, animals, later humans. But not all life could be seen. One early form was like gas—pure energy. That was us: the Lava People."

"Where do they live?"

"In the craters of volcanoes, all over the world. My people lived—still live—on Mount Etna in Sicily."

"Then... how can you live here like this, as a human?"

"I fell in love," she said softly, her smile tinged with sorrow. "With your grandfather. A human. It was forbidden. Lava People do not mix with humans. Our kind punishes such unions. That's why we fled Sicily."

Tuomas hesitated. "If they're invisible... what do they even look like?"

"We can shift our energy at will. I can look human, take the shape of an animal, soar like a bird, even sprout like a flower. But I don't need to change my form—I can make others see what I want. I can influence the brain of any living being."

"Like hypnosis?" Tuomas asked, incredulous.

"You could call it that."

"I'm sorry, Nonna. But this all sounds... impossible. How would someone even know if someone else was like that?"

Nonna's expression darkened. "Do you remember the accident? The one that killed your mother and Uncle Carlo?"

Tuomas looked away. "No. I don't remember anything. Just... waking up in the hospital weeks later."

"Think, Tommaso. The car went up in flames. Your bones were broken, you were unconscious, your clothes were burned. But your skin was untouched—no burns, no smoke in your lungs. Not even your hair was singed."

Tuomas froze.

Nonna's voice dropped to a whisper. "Now you understand. Fire cannot harm a Lava Person."

A rush of buried memories stirred. He remembered doctors whispering when they thought he was asleep—saying his survival made no sense. Some thought he had never been in the car at all. And there was that time at summer camp, in the sauna: the other boys could barely breathe in the steam, while to Tuomas, it felt soft—like sunlight on skin.

"You probably have powers you haven't even discovered yet," Nonna continued. "You must learn to control them—so you won't abuse them."

It sounded like a fantasy. And yet...

Tuomas began to recall other impossible things. The milestone on the beach. The truck crash—hadn't the wall it hit appeared only in his imagination? And the King Kong thing...

"Was Mom like that? Or Uncle Carlo? What about Chiara?"

"No. They weren't. The legacy passes through generations like a sleeping illness—quiet, then fierce. It broke out in you."

She reached up and gently stroked his red hair.

"You are fire-born, Tommaso. You don't burn because you belong to the lava. Poison gas won't kill you. Fire won't touch you. That's how we survive in the craters. And that's only the beginning. Think: what does Chiara take with her when she walks outside at night?"

"A flashlight," Tuomas said slowly.

"And you?"

He paused. "I've never really needed one. I just... see."

"Exactly. Most people stumble in the dark. But not you. Not me. We see like cats. Lava People were born in the shadows of the Earth, where no sun ever reached. Even when we wear a human face, the night belongs to us."

Tuomas's jaw dropped. That was why he could hike the forest paths without tripping. That was why the dark never frightened him. He had just assumed everyone saw the same.

"Are there… more of us?" he asked.

"Yes," she said. "There have always been rebels—Lava People who chose to live among humans. Over thousands of years, many left the craters. Some started families. Their descendants walk among us still. But the legacy only awakens in a few."

"And why do you say 'fortunately'?"

"Because those with awakened powers often rise to greatness. Some become brilliant scientists, athletes, artists. Others, politicians. Leaders. But without understanding their true nature, they grow arrogant. They believe they earned everything alone. They hunger for control. Some of them become cruel. Dictators."

Tuomas leaned forward, heart pounding. "So… some of the worst people in history—were they lava-born?"

Nonna nodded solemnly. "It's possible. You'll learn to recognize them."

"Look at your nonna. Look in the mirror. You will recognize those who are like you."

Although Nonna's body was frail and worn with age, her hair flared like a sea of flames across the pillow—vivid red, without a single gray strand. Her face was etched with deep lines, but her eyes, locked onto Tuomas's, still gleamed with the same sapphire brilliance that lit his own.

Nonna looked tired. Her breathing had grown shallower.

"Did you bring my necklace?" she asked softly.

"I had to take it off at the airport—it kept setting off the metal detector. But I always wear it to remember you."

Tuomas pulled the pendant from his backpack and slipped the cord back around his neck.

"This stone comes from the homeland of my people," Nonna said. "Never give it to anyone. You've probably sensed that it's not just a stone. I'll always be with you, even when I'm no longer here."

"Nonna, don't say that! You're not going to die."

"All people die, Tommaso," she whispered, her voice calm. "But only the body. The spirit you're speaking to now—that will be free. I just can't return to my people, because I chose to live as a human. I hope I'll see my beloved Maurizio again... and our two children, somewhere beyond. The Lava People don't know death. But we humans—who can say what really happens? Every religion tells a different story."

Tuomas blinked away tears. "Did you miss your home? Your family was still there."

Nonna's lips curved into a faint smile. "I made my choice. My family was here. Maurizio, Carlo, Angela, Chiara... and you, Tommaso. You are my family."

From downstairs came the sound of dishes clinking and bursts of laughter. The scent of sizzling steak and fries drifted up through the floorboards. Tuomas's stomach growled audibly.

"Poor Tommaso," Nonna murmured with a faint chuckle. "You're starving after such a long trip. Go eat. Rest.

And tell Sofia I won't be making pasta in the morning—that's her job now."

Just then the door creaked open and Chiara burst in, glowing with excitement. She threw her arms around Tuomas.

"Tommaso! You have to come—dinner's ready! Mom says it's time, and your dad's waiting. Nonna, can I bring you something? Soup? Pasta?"

"Thank you, my dear," Nonna said with a tired smile. "But I don't need anything. I'm just happy Tommaso came."

Chiara took Tuomas's hand and tugged him toward the door. He hesitated. He turned back one last time.

"Nonna… I still have so many questions."

She lifted a hand slowly in farewell.

It was the last time Tuomas saw her alive.

Later that night, when Tuomas and his father had settled into their room, Tuomas realized he had left his tablet on Nonna's bedside table. He thought about going back, but didn't want to wake her—she was probably asleep. Oddly, the tablet had turned itself off.

The next morning, when Nonna didn't appear in the kitchen as usual to start the pasta, Sofia went to check on her. She found her lying peacefully in bed. Gone—just as she'd said she would go.

Tuomas tried to be brave, but tears ran freely down his cheeks. Chiara collapsed in sobs. The two cousins retreated to Chiara's room, away from the noise and tension of the adults.

Sofia called the doctor to certify the death and contacted the funeral home. A long, black car came to carry Nonna's

169

body away from La Colombaia. As it pulled out of the gravel drive, a mournful cry rose from behind the house— old Bruno, the family's watchful hound, howling into the morning.

36

Tuomas picked up the laptop from Nonna's bedside table and clutched it to his chest. "Nonna… you promised to tell me everything," he whispered through trembling lips. "You can't leave me now."

Chiara stood beside him, eyes red and swollen. "What did she tell you?" she asked, her voice cracking.

"Lots of things… things meant only for me," Tuomas replied. "But now she's gone, and I'll never know the rest."

But Nonna had, in her way, kept her promise.

Later, when Tuomas played back the voice recording—using headphones so no one else could hear her secrets—he realized something astonishing: Nonna had kept talking after he left the room. Her voice was faint, the pauses between words so long he kept thinking the recording was over. Then came a sigh. A cough. And her voice, continuing as if he were still sitting at her bedside.

But now, he couldn't ask her questions anymore. She was gone.

"Tommaso," she said softly in the recording, "I know this will be hard for you to believe—but the Lava People are real. As real as humans. Where humans are fleeting… we are eternal."

She sounded proud. There was a long silence. Then another breath, and her voice continued.

"All the volcanoes on Earth are connected through ancient cave systems—so are the Lava People. You young ones have your Internet. We have the 'Volcano Network.' My parents—what you would call parents—were the leaders of our people at Mount Etna. Like a royal couple, you might say. Which made me… a princess. And you, Tommaso, as my grandson, would be something like a prince."

Tuomas yanked the headphones from his ears. A lava prince? Him? Why not a king? His kingdom… was a volcano?

He shook his head, then quickly rewound the file, heart pounding, and pressed play again.

"…a prince," her voice said again. "Sometimes we watched the lives of humans, out of curiosity. But it was forbidden to make contact. I was trusted because of my lineage—I was allowed to linger on the volcanic slopes. I'd take the form of a cat and sit on windowsills, watching families eat together. I'd drop peaches or olives from trees and laugh when people wondered where they'd come from.

"It was on one of those wanderings that I met Maurizio. His family had a house on Etna's slope. He was beautiful—so full of life. And even though I wasn't human… I fell in love. I wanted to live with him. To live as a human. But that was forbidden.

"Our kind must never mix with humans. It would be… unnatural. Like a human marrying a gorilla. I thought I was being careful. But someone saw me.

"The Lava People decided to kill Maurizio—and destroy the valley—to erase the shame that one of us could love a mortal."

Tuomas's hands tightened into fists.

"When the mountain erupted, and lava began to pour down the slopes, I ran to Maurizio's home. It was empty. I protected it with everything I had. When Maurizio returned, I was there—waiting. My hair burned like molten gold. He loved me too. I convinced him to leave with me, to go far away. To live in hiding.

"Here, at La Colombaia, I became human. Angela and Carlo were ordinary children. But you, Tommaso… you are one of us. Which means you're always in danger. My people will want you back. I'll explain why, someday.

"But for now, remember this: Trust no one. Ever. This is our secret. Tell no one."

Her last words were a breathy whisper:

"I need to rest… I'm so tired… Ah, Maurizio, mio caro! Aspetta… aspetta…"

Then only silence.

The ticking of the bedside clock. Bruno's quiet whimpering through the open window.

Nonna's voice faded into eternity.

Tuomas lay on his bed, staring up at the ceiling, his chest tight with grief. Her story played over and over in his mind. It was all too much. The Lava People. Their powers. Their hatred of humans. Her forbidden love. And now, the warning—that they might come for him.

He remembered her words: that they could take any form, seen or unseen. That they wielded tremendous powers. What if he couldn't control his own? What if he hurt someone?

The thought chilled him to the bone.

There was no one left to guide him. No one who knew the truth—except him. Maybe if he just forgot everything, if he deleted the recording and buried the memory, he could go back to being a normal boy.

He made up his mind.

He opened the laptop, hovered over the file—and deleted it.

Especially Chiara, he thought. She would poke her nose into everything. She must never hear it.

Nonna's funeral was simple. Quiet. She had never been one to mingle, not even with the church choir, though Father Alberto had asked her many times to join.

The inheritance had been decided while she was still alive—La Colombaia now belonged to Sofia, Carlo's widow. No one was surprised.

But then came the shock.

Among Nonna's papers was an official will. She had left a house in Sicily—to Tuomas.

The adults looked at one another. Until that moment, no one had mentioned the Costa family's Sicilian past.

The house had once belonged to Maurizio's family. Then to Maurizio. Then to Olivia.

Now, Tuomas was the rightful heir.

Sofia did not contest it. After half a century, the house was probably nothing but crumbling stone. She had enough on her plate managing La Colombaia.

But Tuomas couldn't help but wonder.

What kind of house had survived fifty years of silence?

And what, if anything, was waiting for him in the shadows of Mount Etna?

37

After the reading of the will, Olli Arkko decided it would be best to settle the inheritance issue in Sicily while they were still in Italy. But that meant either hiring a lawyer—or traveling to Sicily themselves.

A trip might do Tuomas good after Nonna's passing. Besides, the boy already seemed deeply curious about Sicily and the house that had once belonged to his grandparents. When Olli brought up the idea, Tuomas lit up immediately, diving into research on his tablet.

"Did you know Mount Etna is the highest volcano in Europe—over 3,300 meters?" Tuomas said, eyes wide with fascination. "Imagine if it erupted while we were there!"

"That's what a lot of tourists hope for," his father grinned. "The thrill of a lifetime."

"Etna formed 500,000 years ago," Tuomas went on. "People still live on its slopes because the lava usually flows slowly—you can outrun it. Unless it's a pyroclastic eruption—those tear down the mountain like express trains, burning everything in their path."

"Sounds charming," Olli chuckled. "Let's hope we catch it on a slow day."

Tuomas tapped his screen. "In 1669, a massive fissure opened in Etna's side and lava flowed all the way to the city of Catania. It reached the port after the city walls gave way. Etna's erupted many times since. In 1929, the whole town of Mascali was buried in lava. But people had time to get out because the flow moved so slowly."

"Good thing we don't have volcanoes, floods, avalanches, or hurricanes in Finland. Almost boring," Olli said with a wink.

Tuomas grinned. "Millions of years ago, there were volcanoes in Finland too. The whole country was covered in lava."

"Glad we were born a little later," his father said with a laugh.

Tuomas paused, the gears turning in his head. Could the Lava People have lived in Finland too?

"The house Nonna left is near Mascali," he said. "I couldn't find the exact address on Google Maps, but the town still exists. I'm sure we can find it."

"There might be old property records in the town archives," Olli suggested.

"It's so strange," Tuomas said quietly. "To think Nonno and Nonna actually lived there."

Then, without warning, he added, "Father… did you know we're all basically passengers—like on a ferry?"

Olli raised an eyebrow. "What? I get seasick, you know."

Tuomas smiled. "The Earth's crust is made of tectonic plates, floating on molten rock. And right where Etna is, two of those plates crash into each other. That's what makes it erupt."

"You're becoming an Etna expert," Olli said with a proud smile. It was good to see Tuomas focusing on something beyond his grief. For Olli, geology held little appeal—his interest in the planet started at 30,000 feet, where the world looked clean and clear from the cockpit of an airliner.

The past left little trace on the land. Lush forests now cloaked Etna's lower slopes. The villages and towns, including Mascali, had been rebuilt. People had returned. Gardens flourished. The volcanic soil—an ancient mix of ash and lava—was rich and fertile.

Higher up, where the lava had hardened into dark flows, only patches of grass and low shrubs took root. In winter, snow blanketed the slopes, and a ski lift ran up the mountainside. Tourists drove to a restaurant near the summit, parking their cars and hiking the final stretch to the smoking crater.

Descending into the crater was strictly forbidden. Still, every year a few thrill-seekers attempted it—and paid the price. Rescue teams with gas masks and ropes had to retrieve them. The gases rising from the cracks were invisible but lethal—unlike the soft white smoke that had drifted from the summit for centuries.

On one slope, set apart from the restaurant and hiking trails, stood a single stone house. Its slate roof and gray walls blended into the rocky landscape. Only the dense, unruly garden revealed its presence. A small stream ran through the overgrown yard. Tall stone walls enclosed it on three sides. It was a haven for animals—but the villagers kept their distance. Even hunters avoided the place and warned hikers not to go near it.

The reasons were always vague, steeped in superstition.

La sposa del vulcano—the bride of the volcano.

La strega di lava—the lava witch.

Gli spiriti malvagi—evil spirits.

Local tour companies had tried several times to buy the house as a rest stop for hikers, but the municipality could never confirm who owned it. The records said the last owners were the Costa family—but they had vanished after an eruption, presumed dead or missing.

Those who dared enter the house came back shaken.

"There's something wrong in there," they said. "The air feels thick—like there's gas. It's hard to breathe. Maybe it's the volcano?" Even the animals seemed strange. Not afraid, but watchful. They stared without blinking... then vanished.

No one picked the fruit from the trees. Ripe apples rotted on the ground, food for rabbits and deer. The olive trees went unharvested, no nets strung below their branches. Vines crept up the house, wild and untamed.

It was as if the land had claimed the house—and the people had agreed to let it.

38

Olli Arkko and Tuomas flew to Sicily. From Catania-Fontanarossa Airport, they took a taxi to the hotel Olli had booked the day before. After a quiet lunch and the usual midday siesta, Olli decided it was time to visit the land registry office in Catania. He had already called ahead before leaving Finland—hoping they could find records about Nonna's house.

He suspected that any property documents lost in the Mascali eruption might have been archived in the provincial capital instead. Luckily, the administrative building was just a few blocks from their hotel.

The moment they stepped out of the cool hotel lobby, the sweltering heat slammed into them like a wave. But a breeze drifting in from the sea offered some relief. The magnolia trees lining the road had finished blooming; their withered pink petals littered the sidewalk like a, fragrant carpet. The air was thick with the sweet scent of orange and lemon trees, drifting from behind high stone garden walls.

As they walked across the Piazza del Duomo, the two paused to admire the palatial baroque buildings the square.

"In Finland, whole towns made of wood have burned down over the centuries," Olli said, shielding his eyes from the sun. "But these buildings have stood here for a thousand years. There's even a Roman amphitheater somewhere nearby. Only an earthquake could take them down."

"Or lava," Tuomas added.

In the distance, the smoky silhouette of Mount Etna loomed over the island. A plume of ash curled lazily into the sky. Tuomas stared at it in silence. Etna... and Nonna's stories. Could any of it be true?

At the land registry office, a grumpy-looking clerk took the folded, yellowed documents from Olli and smoothed them out with visible annoyance before typing in the registration numbers.

"After your call yesterday, I looked into it," he muttered. "I'll check the archive."

He disappeared into a back room. Olli got the sense the man would've preferred to extend his lunch break into dinner, but the unexpected appointment had forced him back to duty.

A few minutes later, the clerk returned with a bundle of maps.

"The records still need to be verified," he said curtly.

"There really shouldn't be any confusion," Olli replied. "The oldest deed I provided shows that the property's been in the Costa family since at least the late 1800s. My son's grandmother left it to him in her will. Here's her death certificate and the official notarized document. If there are any fees or taxes related to the ownership transfer, I'm happy to settle them now."

The clerk glanced at the screen and frowned.

"That area is in a restricted zone. It's classified as a no-build area because it's likely to be buried by lava in a future eruption. It's happened before."

"We're not planning to build anything," Olli explained. "We just want to visit the old family house. That's all. No one's planning to live there."

"There can't be any structures still standing there," the clerk insisted. "The entire region up to Mascali was destroyed. It's just a lava field now. Maybe something has grown back, but that was decades ago."

"There is a house," Tuomas said respectfully, holding out his tablet. "I checked the latest satellite photos on Google. You can see it clearly."

The clerk flushed and began typing furiously. After a few seconds, he stared at the screen in disbelief. He didn't say a word—just picked up the phone and dialed.

Moments later, an older man in a gray jacket stepped into the room, clearly a supervisor. The clerk quickly stood and apologized for disturbing him, gesturing toward the screen and the visitors. The supervisor narrowed his dark eyes and leaned in, reading the data. When he saw the house on the screen, his gaze shifted sharply to Tuomas.

"So you're the new owner of that house?" he asked, voice low and gruff. He turned to the clerk. "Did you check the personal details?"

"Yes, everything's correct. The boy is Finnish—but also Italian, by descent. Dual citizenship."

Olli noticed Tuomas still had his cap on. He tapped him gently on the head—a silent reminder. Tuomas removed the cap.

The moment his red hair caught the light, both officials froze. Their mouths opened slightly, as if they'd seen a ghost.

The supervisor immediately picked up the phone again. Within minutes, several women appeared at the office door. They stopped and stared.

One of them, the oldest, stepped forward, her voice trembling.

"It's true..." she breathed. "My grandmother told me."

Without another word, she turned and walked away quickly, heels clicking on the stone floor. The others followed close behind, whispering to one another in hushed voices. Even the clerk who had helped them disappeared down the corridor.

Tuomas felt a strange knot twist in his stomach.

He wasn't welcome here.

He couldn't explain it, but something inside him already knew why.

Beside him, his father looked increasingly uncomfortable.

"Well," Olli said awkwardly, "what do we do now? Can we register the will and transfer ownership? Is anything missing?"

Tuomas tugged at his father's sleeve. "Maybe... we should go."

"Forget it. Let's go. I don't feel right here."

Tuomas cast a final look at the clerk—direct, steady, as he always did. But the man flinched and raised a hand in front of his face like a shield. A small red dot suddenly shimmered on the back of his hand, as if a laser pointer had landed there. Tuomas blinked. A strange tingling surged behind his eyes, and for a second, a piercing blue-white light seemed to flash across his vision, like the flare of a welding torch. His breath caught in his throat. What... was happening to him?

He closed his eyes and drew a long, slow breath.

"If you thought there was a lot of bureaucracy in Finland," Olli muttered in Finnish, "it's even worse here. And what was with those looks? Like we're from another planet. This place is crawling with tourists every summer."

Tuomas didn't answer. He pulled his cap low over his flaming red hair and stared at the sidewalk.

"Of course, everything is fine," the clerk said from behind the desk, suddenly submissive. "We'll process what you need. No trouble. But… you will have to go to the Mascali town hall. The property technically belongs to their jurisdiction. I'll send them copies of your documents today and let them know you've arrived. Is that acceptable?"

Olli nodded, though still confused. "What kind of trouble could we have possibly caused?" he asked as they stepped back out into the street. "They looked at us like we were mafia. Cosa Nostra or something."

"I'm hungry," Tuomas mumbled, ending the conversation.

That settled it. His father was hungry too.

They walked until they found a cozy pizzeria tucked into a shady corner of downtown. The menu in the window promised all the staples of Mediterranean cuisine, but Tuomas had already made up his mind.

"I just want a pizza," he said.

"Pizza it is," Olli agreed.

They sat at a window table. While waiting for their food, Tuomas glanced up and noticed a man across the street staring directly at him. The man didn't smile or move— just stood there, impassive. Tuomas had taken off his cap before sitting down—no hats at the table, a rule he'd learned in school. Respect the food, the teacher had always said.

He wanted to mention the man to his father, but just then their pizzas arrived, piping hot, with the rich aroma of garlic, basil, and melted cheese. For a moment, everything else faded into the background. By the time Tuomas looked up again, the man was gone.

Later that evening, Olli headed to the hotel bar for a drink, but hesitated at the door.

"You sure you'll be okay alone?" he asked.

"I'm not a baby," Tuomas replied. "We both have phones. I'll just go to bed."

Olli nodded and left.

Tuomas had just undressed and crawled under the covers when his tablet chimed. It was an email from Chiara.

"Two strangers were at the restaurant this morning," she wrote. "I was doing my homework there—it was quiet. They said they were related to Nonna. One of them even had hair like hers. They apologized for missing the funeral, then asked if she had other grandchildren. I showed them that group photo from the memorial. Suddenly they got all excited and took pictures of it with their phones. I told them you and your dad were in Sicily. Then they thanked me and left. Never even had coffee. Weird guys."

Tuomas stared at the message, uneasy. Could that really be a coincidence? Two strangers asking about him... right after Nonna's death?

Trust no one, Nonna had always said.

But he was too tired to dwell on it. Tomorrow they were planning to find Nonna's mountain house, and the heat would make it exhausting. He shut off the light and slipped under the blanket. Thick curtains kept the room in darkness.

He must have dozed off, but a sharp pain in his chest jolted him awake.

Instinctively, he reached beneath his T-shirt. Nonna's stone. It was burning hot—like it had just come out of a fire.

Still half-asleep, Tuomas yanked the chain from his neck. It snapped, and the pendant tumbled onto the bed.

He was wide awake now.

A soft rattle at the door made him freeze.

Father must've forgotten his key card, he thought—but then the door creaked open and clicked shut again. No light came on. A flashlight flickered across the room.

His pulse spiked.

He remembered stories about hotel thieves in the south. Maybe someone thought the room was empty—had watched his father leave and used a spare card to break in.

Two figures slipped inside.

Tuomas's blood ran cold.

Not thieves, he realized. Kidnappers.

"If we sedate him, he won't make noise," one whispered.

"He needs to stay alive. That's what the boss said."

"What if he screams?"

"Then we cover his mouth. No one will hear. We'll wrap him in the blanket."

Tuomas lay perfectly still, barely breathing. His mind raced.

If only Dad were here... but he'd be in danger too. Two against one. I need... I need to disappear.

The men moved closer—one shining a light on the bed, the other holding a cloth that stank of chemicals.

Chloroform, Tuomas realized. He remembered the smell from chemistry class when a bottle had cracked open.

"He's not here!" one hissed.

"Check the bathroom. Under the bed. He couldn't have vanished."

But they couldn't see him.

He was right there, the blanket barely covering his legs —and they didn't see him.

One of the men swept the flashlight over the bed again, cursed under his breath, and snapped, "I told you! Wrong room. You can't even read numbers."

"Let's go. Before someone hears."

They rushed out, slamming the door behind them. The room stank of chloroform.

Tuomas sat up, shaking, every nerve on edge. He stumbled to the window and pushed it open, gulping the cool night air.

Down in the alley, he caught a glimpse of the two men getting into a waiting taxi.

Kidnappers.

And they'd come for him.

He returned to bed, heart still racing. But somewhere between the pounding in his chest and the heat of the stone, a realization settled into place.

He'd wanted to be invisible.

And he had been.

He wasn't just a boy.

He was a lava boy.

When Olli returned, Tuomas pretended to be asleep.

There was no use telling his father. No one would believe it. There were no signs of a break-in, nothing stolen, no proof. Just the reek of chemicals that might as well have been from a cleaning cart.

Olli closed the window and climbed into bed, none the wiser.

Tuomas lay still, eyes wide open in the dark.

A new question stirred inside him.

What else can I do?

39

The next morning, Tuomas found the broken pendant tangled in the sheets. "The chain snapped last night," he said, holding it up. "It must've happened when the stone got so hot. I pulled it off in my sleep."

"There are jewelers here," Olli said. "We'll find someone who can fix it after breakfast."

At the front desk, the receptionist directed them to a nearby jeweler tucked away on a quiet side street. He also jotted down a note for a taxi to Mascali and promised to arrange it for the next morning.

After breakfast, they followed a narrow alley until they found the shop. A faded sign hung above the door. When Tuomas opened it, the bell chimed, and a wheelchair rolled out from behind a curtain. An old man with silver-gray hair sat in it.

"Buongiorno," he greeted them warmly. "What can I do for you?"

Tuomas fished the broken necklace out of his pocket and laid it gently on the glass counter. "The chain broke," he said.

The jeweler picked up the pendant—but quickly set it back down, as if it had burned his fingers. He peered at it, then reached under the counter for a magnifying glass.

"Do you know what kind of stone this is?" he asked, his tone suddenly cautious.

Tuomas shook his head. "No. My grandma gave it to me. She said it would help me remember her. That's why it's so important. I wear it all the time."

The old man nodded slowly. "Very interesting… very interesting indeed…" he murmured, more to himself than to them. Then he retrieved a small device from the display case.

"This is a polarizing microscope," he explained. "It's used to identify gemstones."

"We don't need to identify the stone," Olli said, growing impatient. "We just want the necklace fixed. We're in a bit of a rush."

"Sì, sì, of course," the jeweler said vaguely. "It won't take long… and no charge." But his attention was locked on the stone. He gazed through the microscope, mumbling in Italian, then pulled a thick book from beneath the counter.

Tuomas watched curiously.

"This can't be right… and yet… the inclusions… clearly a hexagonal crystal system…" the old man whispered, flipping through the pages.

"Here, look," he said finally, sliding the microscope toward Tuomas.

Tuomas bent over and peered in. Under magnification, the red flecks in the stone shimmered like stars in a dark sky.

"It's beautiful," he breathed. "What is it?"

"If I'm correct…" The jeweler tapped the book. "This could be taaffeite."

Tuomas blinked. He had never heard of it. The strange name didn't mean anything to him. His excitement deflated. "Oh. Okay," he said. "Well, can you fix the chain so I can wear it again?"

The jeweler looked up, frowning. He turned to Olli. "If I were this boy's father, and he had a stone like this… I'd keep it in a safe. Not around his neck."

"Thanks for the advice," Olli said flatly. "But we're in a hurry."

"Of course. I'll solder it in the back." The old man disappeared behind the curtain, wheels softly squeaking on the floor.

A few minutes later, he returned and handed the repaired necklace to Tuomas, who immediately put it back on and tucked it under his T-shirt.

"Do you know where the stone came from?" the jeweler asked as he handed over the necklace.

Tuomas shrugged. "No idea. I think someone gave it to my nonna."

He was glad it was fixed. He was even more eager to leave—the man from the pizzeria was standing outside again, peering into the shop window.

Was he imagining things? Or seeing ghosts?

Once Tuomas and his father were gone, the doorbell chimed again. The man outside stepped into the shop. The old jeweler dropped his magnifying glass in surprise.

"Hello, Carlo," the man said coolly. "It's been a while."

"It's not payday yet," the jeweler muttered, voice shaky.

"What did the tourists want?" the man demanded.

"They asked me to fix a necklace," the old man replied.

"Was it valuable?"

"Yes… and no."

"No riddles."

"The pendant contained a rare gem. So rare it's not used in jewelry—only found in museums."

"Well, the museum's loss could be the owner's gain. And ours, if there are more like it. Now tell me everything you know."

The man slammed his palm on the counter. The jewelry inside clinked sharply against the glass.

"Did you hear me?" he barked.

"Yes, yes," the jeweler stammered, trembling in his wheelchair. He told the man everything.

"Grazie. You're an old fool... but not a stupid one," the man said, smirking. He stepped behind the counter, up the dropped magnifier, and placed it gently on the glass.

"Addio," he said with mock affection, kissing the jeweler's cheeks before slipping out the door, rubbing his hands together with satisfaction.

Back at the hotel, Olli went to the front desk to settle the bill. They wouldn't be returning.

Tuomas went up to his room and immediately powered on his tablet.

Taaffeite... Taaffeitis... He typed the name into the search bar.

"I thought it was just a normal gemstone. Like ruby or sapphire," he muttered.

But when the page loaded, his eyes widened.

Taaffeite wasn't ordinary at all. It was one of the rarest gems in the world—worth as much as $16,000 per carat. And a carat was only one-fifth of a gram.

Tuomas swallowed hard.

"I'm never telling Dad," he thought nervously. "If he finds out, he'll make me lock it away... maybe even sell it."

He reached under his shirt and pressed the pendant against his chest.

This isn't just a stone, he thought. It's part of who I am.

40

When they stepped out of the hotel, a taxi was already waiting by the curb. Tuomas slid into the back seat while his father spread out a map on the car's hood, pointing out their destination.

"I'll find it," the driver muttered, barely glancing at the map. His cap was pulled low over his forehead, and oversized sunglasses hid his eyes—but his gaze lingered on Tuomas just a little too long.

Olli climbed in beside his son. "At least there's air conditioning," he said with a sigh of relief. "We'd be roasted without it. Should be a pleasant ride."

But the air inside was so cold that Tuomas shivered. Even so, Nonna's pendant—resting against his bare chest —was beginning to warm again. He winced and tugged it over his T-shirt.

Not again, Nonna, he thought, annoyed. Her constant presence was starting to feel more like surveillance than protection.

Mascali was still twenty kilometers away. As the landscape passed by, Tuomas searched for signs of the ancient disaster that had once buried the town in lava—but everything had long since been rebuilt. The houses were soft pastels—peach, rose, pale yellow—with small wrought-iron balconies, like so many other towns in Italy. The tallest structure was the old church, the only building that had survived the eruption.

"We'll visit the church later," Olli said. "First, we've got to sort out the house paperwork at the municipal office."

He added, "It might take a while, but I'll pay the driver to wait."

They pulled up in front of the town hall. Two officers stood on either side of the entrance, but that wasn't unusual. What felt strange was the silence inside.

The corridors were deserted. No employees bustled about, no visitors sat waiting. Every door bore a glowing red "Reserved" sign. Even the front reception desk was unmanned.

Then, from a back hallway, an old cleaning lady shuffled out. Olli greeted her politely, but before he could ask a question, she waved him off with surprising confidence.

"Il dipartimento immobiliare si trova al secondo piano," she said briskly—and disappeared back into the hallway.

Father and son made their way to the second floor, as instructed. The red "Busy" lights still flashed on the office doors, but a jittery-looking clerk stood behind the reception desk of the notary's office.

She didn't ask for ID. All the documents were already laid out, neatly prepared. The transfer of ownership took only a few minutes, the paperwork was signed, and the payment processed swiftly by credit card.

It felt... too easy.

As they descended the steps outside, the two policemen at the door nodded politely. Tuomas glanced back at the city hall. In a few upstairs windows, he could now see people watching them. The important meetings, it seemed, had just ended.

The road to the mountains twisted and climbed, wrapping around the volcanic slope in ever-tightening switchbacks. The palms and vineyards gave way to groves of oaks and beeches, and then to slender birches. They passed walnut trees and scattered almonds. Higher up, the landscape turned harsher—only conifers survived now, and finally, just low, stubborn shrubs clawed their way through the blackened rock.

"Are you sure this is the right place?" Olli asked again, glancing at the driver.

"Sì, signore," the man replied flatly, never looking back.

Eventually, with the villages far below them no more than toy houses in the valley, the taxi pulled into a gravel turnout on the side of the road and stopped.

"We're here," the driver said with a shrug. "Or at least close enough."

Olli got out and stretched, then opened the map on the hot hood of the car. He checked his handwritten notes and compared them to the GPS coordinates on his phone. He also had a compass—he might be grounded now, but the instincts of a pilot still served him well.

"The house should be this way," he said, pointing. "We'll have to hike the rest. It's nearly a kilometer. The old road isn't where it used to be."

Tuomas nodded, already slinging on his backpack. "Of course I can make it," he said, more determined than ever. "We're finally here."

Olli explained to the driver that they would be gone for at least two hours. The man didn't care. He leaned against the side of the cab and lit a cigarette. The smoke curled through the air—sharp and oddly familiar. Tuomas frowned. Did everyone in Sicily smoke the same brand?

They set off along a faint trail that wove through lava rocks, disappearing now and then only to reappear farther ahead. Tuomas kept his eyes on the horizon.

His grandparents had lived here.

This place, harsh and haunting, held his family's roots. And if Nonna's stories were true, then somewhere beneath their feet, hidden deep in the veins of the mountain, the ancient and mysterious Lava People still lived.

His people.

41

I know he's coming. My spies have told me. There are humans who still owe debts to the Lava People. Perhaps we saved them after they slipped into the crater's edge. Perhaps we helped them find the glittering stones they covet so dearly.

But the Lava People never forgive those who abandon us. To leave is betrayal. To leave is disgrace. We do not welcome the traitors back—they would defile our eternal homeland. No. We do not forgive. We take revenge.

When my daughter fell in love with that insignificant human boy, we razed the valley. We buried the towns and villages in molten fire. We chased the humans away with eruptions, with lava and ash. But I could not destroy my daughter—she was a part of me, as I was a part of her. Nor could I reach her. He had already fled, unaware she loved him. Unaware that all that death and ruin had been for him.

They escaped. Far enough that my power could no longer touch them.

As is our custom, I should have taken their firstborn in her place. But neither of her children—first the girl, then the boy—was born within the Lava Line.

They were... anomalies. Unworthy. There was no to bring them back. No claim to make.
But now... everything has changed.
My great-grandson is a true child of the lava. It is in his blood. In his bones. Not only his flaming hair—but his power. His presence. He carries our gifts, even if he doesn't yet understand them.
I will bring the boy back to my kingdom. All these years, I preserved the house—kept it standing when the rest of the mountain crumbled—so it would call to him. So it would pull him to me.
And now... He comes.

The path ended abruptly. Jagged stones and hardened lava had formed a natural wall, beyond which a grove of tall olive trees swayed in the breeze. Tuomas and his father followed the wall until they reached a rusted iron gate set into the stone. Beyond it lay a lush garden, overgrown but alive—and at its center stood a low house made of flat lava stones, dark and solid like it had grown straight from the mountain.

"Should we go in?" Olli asked, hesitating. "Maybe someone lives here. And not everyone around here likes strangers poking around. People can be... odd."

Tuomas didn't answer. He pulled out his tablet, held it above the gate, and started filming.

Through the screen, he saw the door to the house slowly creak open—and a dark figure stepped into view.

At the same time, Olli pushed open the gate with a creak of old iron hinges.

Then something leapt from the shadows—fast, massive, and silent.

A large, dark-gray animal lunged from beneath the trees, its eyes wild. A chain snapped taut around its neck just in time, stopping it only a few feet from the gate. The beast let out a guttural growl and strained upward as if trying to tear free.

Tuomas and Olli stumbled back, hearts pounding.

The animal snarled, its ears flattened, its tail low and stiff. It looked like a dog—but also, somehow, like a wolf. Whatever it was, it clearly didn't want them getting any closer.

"There's no way we're getting to that house," Olli muttered, edging backward.

But Tuomas didn't move. He stared at the animal, thinking. What could scare it? And then an image came to him: a bear. A massive Finnish bear, upright like a king of the forest—something primal, powerful.

He met the animal's gaze without flinching.

What do you see? he thought. Do you see me… or something else?

The growling stopped. The creature blinked, its posture softening. It lowered its ears and slowly backed away into the garden, the heavy chain dragging in the dirt.

"What the hell just happened?" Olli asked, stunned.

Tuomas said nothing. He didn't have to. The explanation came a moment later.

From the doorway of the house, a stooped woman in a long black skirt appeared. Her head was wrapped in a dark scarf, her face lined and sun-worn. But her voice, when she spoke, was kind.

"Excuse my dog. We don't get many visitors up here."

"We didn't mean to intrude," Olli said quickly. "We weren't sure the house was still occupied. The city office didn't even think it existed."

"The men in the city don't care about such things," the woman replied calmly, eyeing them both with a quiet intensity.

Olli explained the reason for their visit—that his son had inherited the property.

"I suppose you're wondering what I'm doing here," the woman said, without waiting for the question.

"As far as we know, there are no living heirs in Sicily," Olli said cautiously, uneasy with this unexpected turn.

"I'm a distant relative of the family who once lived here. After the eruption, when the owner and his wife were lost, someone from our line always took care of the house. If we hadn't, the tourists would've claimed it—or the locals would've carried it away stone by stone to build sheepfolds."

Olli glanced around, taking in the dense, thriving olive grove. "It's strange," he said. "Everything around this place is green and alive, but outside the wall—it's just barren rock."

The woman smiled faintly. "Nature has moods of its own. But tell me—what will you do with the house? Do you plan to live here?"

Her smile sharpened slightly. There was something schievous about it.

"We haven't thought that far ahead," Olli said. "Right, Tuomas?"

Tuomas said nothing. He was watching the woman refully.

She seemed kind. Harmless, even. But something in him stayed alert.

Trust no one, Nonna had always said.

And now, under his shirt, the pendant burned hot against his skin.

The woman raised her head and met his gaze. Her eyes were deep sapphire blue—just like Nonna's. Or… like his own.

She knew.

"It's a hot day to climb the mountain," she said softly. "Come inside. Rest. Maybe even spend the night. After all… it's your house."

Nonna's voice echoed in his mind again.

Trust no one.

"Thank you," Olli replied, "but our taxi's waiting. We've seen what we needed to see. What do you say, Tuomas?"

Tuomas let out a quiet breath. "Let's go back. We'll come another time. It's good someone's been looking after the place. It really is beautiful."

The woman nodded, her eyes still fixed on him.

"You're always welcome," she said. "This house is yours. By right."

They turned to leave. As they started down the path, Olli paused and looked back.

"Excuse me," he called. "We never got your name."

The woman let out a dry, gentle laugh.

"Names?" she said. "Names are just smoke and mirrors… things people make up."

And as they disappeared around the curve of the path, the woman reached up and pulled off her scarf.

Flaming red hair tumbled free, gleaming like fire in the sunlight.

My great-grandson carries the power of our people. Not a flicker. Not a trace. He is imbued—completely. My husband and I gave a portion of our strength to our daughter. But in him... it has awakened fully. He will become a skilled leader, a true heir to the Lava People.

I will bring him back. It is his destiny.

He defeated Lupo, yes—but it was mere instinct. A reflex. A raw, unconscious surge he doesn't yet understand. But he has been warned. My daughter must have told him something... before she passed.

Curiosity will pull him back.

And I— I can wait.

We, the Lava People, are eternal. Time means nothing to us.

42

Strange woman, Olli thought, as they made their way back up the slope to the road. Tuomas walked in silence. Too much had happened in the past few days—too many strange things he still didn't understand.

"I don't want to keep the house," Tuomas said abruptly. "We should try to sell it."

"Let's think about it when we get home," Olli replied, slowing his pace. "There's no rush."

"Do you want to take the taxi a bit closer to the crater?" he offered after a moment. "We've come all this way— might as well see the top of Etna."

Tuomas nodded. He was curious too. They were nearly at the summit, after all.

But just then, the ground trembled beneath their feet. A strange pressure moved through their bodies, as if the very earth had exhaled. Stones tumbled from the slope, bouncing across the dusty trail.

"We should leave," Olli said quickly, his voice low and firm.

Their taxi was still waiting, just as promised. The driver sat in the shade beside the car, smoking. Judging by the pile of cigarette butts at his feet, he had gone through most of the pack. He stood up and flicked the half-smoked cigarette onto the ground.

"I have to smoke because of the wasps," he explained, unprompted. "They're still up here—buzzing around the trash. I'm allergic. If I get stung, I need an injection right away."

It was the longest sentence the driver had spoken during the entire trip.

"Did you gentlemen find your view?" he asked as he opened the back door for them.

"Seen everything," Olli replied shortly.

Tuomas felt a strange sense of relief as the car pulled away from the mountain and descended toward the valley. It was time to go. Their flight from Catania-Fontanarossa Airport was scheduled for that very afternoon. The tickets were booked, the seats reserved, and they shared a single suitcase for check-in. Olli carried a small bag for hand luggage. Tuomas had his backpack.

After check-in, there was still time for a snack—a sandwich and a cold beer for Olli, an ice-cold Coke for Tuomas. The flight would be over five hours, and there would be a meal on board. While his father leafed through the thick envelope of documents from the notary, Tuomas pulled out his tablet.

He wanted to rewatch the video he had taken of Nonna's house.

But when the footage began to play, Tuomas froze.

He saw the house. The garden. The front door opened—but no one came out.

No black-clad woman. No soft voice. Nothing. The figure he had clearly seen approaching them was invisible in the video.

How is that possible? Tuomas thought. I saw her. We both saw her. She spoke to us. Father even answered her.

But the camera—just a machine—had recorded nothing.

Was she a ghost? Or something else? Something with power over light, over perception—like Nonna?

"What are you watching?" Olli asked, noticing his son's furrowed brow.

"I took a quick video of Nonna's house—for Chiara. But it didn't turn out very well."

"Let me see," Olli said, reaching for the tablet. He watched the video and nodded. "Looks fine to me. It's a nice house. Maybe we'll go back someday. Take Chiara along."

He didn't seem to notice that the front door opened by itself.

Tuomas breathed easier.

When boarding was finally announced, Tuomas felt a wave of relief. Sicily had been beautiful, yes—but also strange. Hot. Intense. The streets shimmered in the heat, and the asphalt had looked like it was about to melt. He longed for the cool spring air of Finland.

He had hoped to return to La Colombaia in the summer, to see his Italian relatives again—but his father had refused. Chiara was still in school, and after Nonna's death, everything felt different. The tourist season had begun, and Tuomas would've been a distraction.

Besides, his father wanted to spend the summer with him in Finland. Just the two of them.

The plane was full—businessmen in dark suits, sweaty backpackers, and cheerful Japanese tourists who snapped pictures of everything, even the boarding stairs. At one point, the line came to a halt because they'd asked a flight attendant to take a group photo.

While they waited, Tuomas glanced toward the front of the line—and froze again.

The taxi driver.

He was there, among the passengers. But this time, he wasn't wearing his cap and jacket. He wore a loud Hawaiian shirt and oversized sunglasses. The disguise might have worked… if not for the thick black mustache and greasy hair spilling over his collar.

Tuomas recognized him instantly.

Before he could say anything to his father, the line moved again. The Japanese tourists finished their photo, and the rest of the passengers were finally allowed to board. The man disappeared into the crowd.

Tuomas and his father had seats by the emergency exit. His backpack had to go in the overhead bin, but Olli promised to hand him the tablet as soon as they were in the air.

Tuomas nodded.

He wanted to send Chiara the photos of Nonna's old house.

Even if something—or someone—had stayed hidden in the shadows.

43

The plane took off on time, banking gracefully out over the sea. The landing gear retracted with a muffled thump, and the seatbelt sign blinked off. Tuomas barely noticed. He'd flown so often that the sounds were familiar, almost comforting.

But then the aircraft began to turn.

His father frowned. "Are they flying around a storm system?"

For a while, the plane had been cruising over open water, but now it appeared to be circling back—toward Sicily. No announcement came. Most passengers were too distracted by vacation photos on their phones and tablets to notice.

As the seatbelt sign remained off, Olli unbuckled. Curious and concerned—instincts from years in the cockpit—he got up to speak to a flight attendant.

But before he could take a step, a man jumped up from the front row, brandishing a machine gun.

"Resta seduto o sparo!" he shouted. Stay seated or I'll shoot!

He wore a black hood, but Tuomas instantly recognized the Hawaiian shirt beneath it.

The taxi driver.

The seatbelt signs blinked back on, and a voice crackled over the intercom—not the friendly tone of the captain who had welcomed them before takeoff.

"This flight has been hijacked. We are being diverted to a new destination. Please remain calm and fasten your seatbelts."

Tuomas's heart skipped a beat. He gripped his father's hand tightly as Olli obeyed and sat down beside him.

The hooded man's gaze locked on Tuomas through the eyeholes in his mask.

This is about me, Tuomas realied. They're here for me.

"Don't worry," his father whispered, squeezing his hand. "We'll be fine."

There were at least two hijackers—one armed in the cabin, and another in the cockpit, forcing the pilots to change course. The flight attendants had been ordered to the front and strapped into their jump seats, pale with fear.

A wave of panic rippled through the passengers. The Japanese tourists had finally noticed the gunman, and now there were shouts and screams. A baby cried somewhere near the back of the plane.

"Silenzio!" the hijacker barked, swinging the gun. One passenger cowered as the muzzle passed inches from his face.

Tuomas leaned toward his father. "Where are they going?"

"We're flying low," Olli muttered. "Too low. If they don't pull up soon…"

Tuomas looked out the window. The dark ridgeline of Etna was approaching fast.

The volcano. They were flying toward the crater.

Tuomas's blood turned cold. Was this some twisted suicide mission? Was he really that important?

The hijacker's eyes found his again. That cold, fixed stare. Tuomas fought to keep breathing. A sudden itch tickled the back of his neck. A mosquito? He didn't dare move.

Then he remembered: the taxi driver had complained about wasps near the trash. He had said he was allergic. A single sting could send him into shock.

Can I... create something? Tuomas thought. Can I make him believe the wasps are back?

He focused, concentrating harder than ever before. He imagined the buzzing. The panic. The stings.

Suddenly, the hijacker jerked upright. He began flailing wildly, swatting at invisible attackers.

"Via! Aiuto!" he screamed, swiping the air around his face. His gun waved erratically.

People ducked and screamed. The man tore off his hood, revealing his contorted face, red and swollen with panic.

"I need a doctor!" he cried, gasping for breath. "The wasps—I'm allergic—I'll die!"

He stumbled toward the cockpit, banging on the door with the butt of his weapon. "Open up! We have to land!"

The door opened—and the co-pilot emerged, revolver in hand.

So he's the second hijacker, Tuomas realized.

"What are you doing?" the co-pilot asked coldly.

"They're stinging me—I need help!" the hijacker wheezed, clutching his neck.

The co-pilot sneered. "Then die. We don't need you anymore. We're almost there."

He shoved the hijacker away and turned back to the cockpit.

But at that moment, something heavy crashed into the back of his head.

The co-pilot crumpled.

A flight attendant stood behind him, her face blazing with fury, a red fire extinguisher clenched in her hands.

"You bastard," she shouted. "You traitor! You were going to kill us—you're one of us!"

She raised the extinguisher again.

"Enough!" Olli stepped forward and pulled her back before she could strike again. He turned the unconscious co-pilot onto his stomach and called for zip ties.

One of the other flight attendants rummaged through the emergency kit and handed them over. With quick, practiced hands, Olli restrained both hijackers. The taxi driver didn't resist—he was still gasping, shaking, stunned. But Tuomas knew the truth:

There were no wasps.

Only he knew they had never existed.

The passengers erupted in applause, relief crashing through the cabin like a wave. But Olli didn't relax.

"We're still flying in the wrong direction," he said grimly. "And too low. Why hasn't the captain corrected course?"

The flight attendant opened the cockpit door and stepped inside. A moment later, she reappeared, pale.

"The captain…" she said softly. "He's collapsed."

Olli rushed forward. The captain sat slumped in his seat, head in his hands.

"My head…" he groaned faintly.

"He's had a brain hemorrhage before," the attendant whispered, eyes wide. "He shouldn't have flown. And now—now we're all going to—"

"No," Olli interrupted. Calm. Focused. "We're not."

With quiet determination, he gently moved the captain to the floor. Then he slid into the pilot's seat, slipped on the headset, and gripped the controls.

The volcano loomed ahead.

There was no time to lose.

"Altitude first," Olli muttered. "We're flying over that mountain."

44

Tuomas didn't know exactly what was happening in the cockpit, but he could feel the engines roar louder as the plane rapidly gained altitude. The sudden climb sent a sharp pain through his ears, and passengers around him screamed. Some jumped up in panic, losing their balance and toppling into their neighbors' laps.

In the midst of the chaos, a man moved swiftly down the aisle—unnoticed until it was too late.

He reached Tuomas's row and, without warning, yanked him out of his seat. Tuomas was dragged from the window seat into the aisle. The man's hand clamped around his arm like a vice as he lunged toward the emergency exit.

Panic erupted.

Tuomas's eyes widened in horror. As the son of a pilot, he knew exactly what would happen if the door was opened mid-flight—at this altitude, the sudden decompression and rushing air would suck them out instantly.

The man worked with terrifying speed and precision. He knew what he was doing. Within seconds, the emergency hatch was open—and a howling vortex of wind tore through the cabin.

Outside, the volcano loomed below.

The man turned to Tuomas, his eyes cold behind the wind-whipped strands of hair, and said with a chilling smile:

"Well, little prince… time to enter your kingdom."

Then he jumped—dragging Tuomas with him.

They fell.

For a moment, there was no up or down, only whirling sky and smoke and wind tearing at Tuomas's clothes and hair. The man's grip on his arm was iron. The earth spun below, the smoking crater of Mount Etna rushing toward them.

This is how I die, Tuomas thought, numb with fear. Poor Dad…

Then, he felt a tug—his arm wrenched painfully—and the man was gone.

Tuomas was falling alone.

High above, a parachute had deployed. The man had let go. He hadn't planned to die after all. He had stashed the parachute in his backpack. His real plan had been to throw Tuomas into the volcano and float safely away.

Tuomas tumbled through the air, helpless.

The pendant around his neck whipped upward and brushed against his face. Nonna's stone. Did he really have powers? Was there still time to use them?

I'm falling because I'm human, Tuomas thought. But what if I weren't? If I had wings… if I were a bird…

He pictured a seagull gliding over the lake near his home in Finland. The way its wings caught the wind. The way it floated, light as air.

He closed his eyes—and something changed.

The wind no longer tore at him. It lifted him.

His arms were wings. His body weightless. Feathers spread wide and glimmering in the sun. He wasn't fall-ing—he was flying.

Tuomas had become a bird.

An overwhelming rush of joy surged through him. He soared higher, banking left, then right, catching thermals as though he'd flown his whole life. Beneath him, the crater loomed—but with a few powerful wingbeats, he rose above it.

Then he saw it—his sharp bird vision picking out a flash of color in the dark.

The kidnapper's parachute.

It had landed inside the volcano. Crumpled on the rocks near the crater's edge. The man had missed his mark—or perhaps the toxic gases had disoriented him. Without a gas mask, he never stood a chance. He wasn't moving.

Tuomas felt no pity. No one had forced him to become a kidnapper.

Still, Tuomas had a problem. The plane was long gone, flying east over the sea. His father—and their luggage— were aboard. He had no passport, no money, no backpack.

I have to get back to the airport.

He remembered the map he had studied with his father. From the sky, the highways that led to Catania were easy to spot. The airport was only a few miles away.

Flying felt incredible. Natural. As if he'd been born to do it. But with that power came fear: What if I suddenly change back? Midair?

This is what Nonna meant, he realized. You have to learn to control your powers.

As long as his wings held him, he'd stay aloft—but he wouldn't risk it forever.

Meanwhile, back on the plane, Olli had pulled the aircraft up just in time to clear the volcano. The passengers were shaken, the cabin still in chaos, but they were safe— for now.

In the cockpit, air traffic control had ordered a return to Catania-Fontanarossa.

One of the flight attendants, still shaking, listened intently to a doctor on the line from the airport's medical team. They were giving instructions on how to care for the incapacitated captain, who had collapsed moments earlier.

Together, she and her colleague carefully laid the man on the floor. His breathing was shallow but steady.

Olli stayed at the controls. Steady hands. Focused mind. He couldn't think about anything else—not even his missing son.

Not yet.

The police had to be briefed on how to handle the once in custody. Injured passengers—those who had fallen during the violent flight—also required immediate medical attention.

In all the confusion, the sudden opening of the emergency exit had gone almost unnoticed. The alarm had gone off, yes—but with everyone focused on regaining control of the plane, it hadn't registered as urgent. With the help of a few strong passengers, a flight attendant had eventually managed to force the door shut again.

When the plane landed—Olli bringing it in with the calm precision of a seasoned pilot—armed police immediately surrounded the aircraft. Ambulances, fire trucks, and police cars swarmed the tarmac in a blur of flashing lights.

The hijackers and those needing medical care were removed first. Only after that were the remaining passengers allowed to disembark.

Olli remained in the cockpit, steady and alert—until a flight attendant leaned in.

"There was an incident during the flight," she said. "Someone opened the emergency exit midair. A passenger may have jumped."

Olli's stomach dropped.

"My son," he said quickly. "He was seated by that exit. Tuomas. What happened to my son?"

The flight attendants looked at each other helplessly. None of them had witnessed it directly—they had been busy restraining the hijackers and assisting the injured captain.

Olli stepped out of the cockpit and scanned the line of disembarking passengers. He looked for the unmistakable flash of red hair.

Nothing.

Then, a polite voice stopped him.

A Japanese tourist bowed slightly and said in accented English, "I am very sorry about your son. He... he jumped. With that man. The one in the Hawaiian shirt."

"What?" Olli's voice cracked. "What do you mean, he jumped?"

"The man pulled the boy from his seat. They opened the door. We saw a parachute. It deployed. So maybe... maybe they survived."

The passenger bowed again and moved on.

Olli stood frozen.

Tuomas's blue backpack was later found on the overhead shelf. But there was no sign of Tuomas himself.

The airport operation—already overwhelmed by the hijacking—shifted into overdrive.

Olli coordinated the launch of a rescue helicopter and multiple search patrols. He supplied them with a copy of Tuomas's passport photo and described his bright red hair. Flyers were printed. Images were sent to police and emergency workers across the region.

The man in the Hawaiian shirt—the presumed skydiver—was listed on the passenger manifest. But the identity could have been forged. Perhaps he was one of the hijackers. That, they hoped, would become clear after interrogating the two arrested men.

One was suffering from a severe concussion after being knocked unconscious with a fire extinguisher. The other, still bloated and gasping for breath, claimed he'd been attacked by a swarm of wasps midair—though no stings could be found. His skin was bright red, as if he'd been boiled.

Despite his condition, he angrily threatened to sue the airline for "releasing dangerous pests" and putting passengers at risk.

In a low-flying helicopter, Olli sat beside the pilot, scanning the volcanic terrain with binoculars. Every inch of the landscape below was hostile—craggy lava flows, sharp ridges, fields of blackened stone. If the parachutist had landed on the upper slopes, the parachute might be visible. But if Tuomas had fallen separately—if he had landed unconscious somewhere in the dense vegetation of the lower forests—he could be impossible to find.

Why had the man taken Tuomas with him? What did he want?

Olli couldn't believe it was random. The stranger hadn't just kidnapped his son. He had planned this. He had waited until the last moment.

The same question gnawed at him: Why?

And then, another thought twisted in his chest like a knife: Had he lost him?

Had he lost the only person in the world worth living for?

Memories came flooding back—of that day in the Emirates, when he'd crash-landed a private jet in the desert after engine failure. He'd pulled Abdullah's eldest son from the wreckage just before it went up in flames. Everyone had called him a hero. But what good were heroics now, when his own son had vanished from the sky?

He gripped the binoculars tighter and kept searching.

Please, Tuomas. Let me find you. Just one sign. Please.

45

Half a dozen armed officers—Carabinieri—stood at the entrance to the airport parking lot, checking driver's licenses and watching every passenger who entered or exited the terminal. High above them, Tuomas circled like a seagull, scanning for a safe place to land.

After everything that had happened, he was exhausted—and desperate to find a restroom. But seagulls had no such concerns. Instead, something white splattered directly onto a policeman's cap.

His colleague burst out laughing and pointed to the mess. The officer pulled off his cap, stared at the fresh seagull droppings, and flushed with anger. What nerve! An insult to the police—an act of terrorism!

When the laughing officer pointed at the bird overhead, the furious policeman drew his pistol and started shooting. The others, startled by the sudden gunfire, assumed it was an attack and joined in. The deafening crack of bullets filled the air. Panicked passengers ducked behind cars.

Tuomas barely escaped, diving behind a van and shifting back into human form just in time.

"We got it!" one of the officers cheered. "We got the damn bird!"

But when they rushed over to confirm the kill, they found—not a bird—but a disoriented, slightly scraped-up boy with blazing red hair crouching behind the van.

"Hey… isn't this the kid the whole island's looking for?" one officer said.

He checked the boy's breast pocket. There it was: a copy of Tuomas's passport, distributed earlier to search teams.

"Tu sei... you are Tuoo...mas?" the officer asked hesitantly.

Tuomas nodded.

In an instant, he was surrounded by the Carabinieri and marched—more dragged than escorted—toward the airport's administrative wing.

Meanwhile, Olli was still circling the volcano in a rescue helicopter, scanning the crater through binoculars. They stayed at a safe altitude above the active caldera. On the rocky floor below, the parachute was clearly visible—tangled and motionless.

Olli's heart pounded. Was that where Tuomas had landed? Was he trapped beneath the fabric? Was he—

"There's no movement," the pilot reported.

"I want a descent team," Olli ordered. "We need to land. Rappel down if we have to."

"Sir, there are sulfur emissions. We'll need gas masks, and—"

But the pilot's radio suddenly crackled.

A voice from air traffic control came through, urgent and clear:

"The boy has been found. He's alive. He's at the airport."

Olli froze. Then he slumped forward, letting out a deep, shuddering breath. Tears filled his eyes. The crew let out a cheer, clapping one another on the back, their faces lit with disbelief.

A miracle.

Back at the airport, Olli burst into the control office and found his son surrounded by five heavily armed policemen.

"Dad!" Tuomas cried, and ran into his arms.

They held each other tightly, unmoving. For a long moment, the rest of the room didn't exist.

Then a uniformed officer stepped forward and cleared his throat.

"Signore Arkko, we have many questions for you and your son. The situation is… highly unusual."

Olli looked up, still holding Tuomas close.

The officer continued, "Reports are contradictory. Some say there were multiple hijackers—including a flight attendant. Another claims the hijacker shot the captain and jumped. A third says you, Signore Arkko, single-handedly subdued a gang of hijackers and saved the plane. And now your son, who supposedly fell from the sky, turns up walking into the airport like nothing happened. This makes no sense."

Olli turned to Tuomas. "How did you survive? How did you get here?"

Tuomas hesitated, then said simply, "I landed on the side of the volcano. A van picked me up and brought me to the airport."

That was all he offered.

The lead officer frowned.

"And the man you jumped with—did you know him? Witnesses say you fell together."

"I don't know who he was," Tuomas said. "When I woke up, he was gone."

Just then, the airport doctor entered the room.

"I'd like to take the boy to the hospital," he said firmly. "A fall—or jump—like that could cause internal injuries or a concussion. He needs observation at the very least."

The officer looked ready to object, but finally nodded. "Very well. But we'll need a full statement from both of you."

Tuomas was gently lifted onto a stretcher. As they wheeled him away, he murmured, half amused:

"What would they have done if I really had been injured?"

The doctor smiled. "Let's not find out."

One of the officers turned to Olli.

"Signore Arkko, please accompany us to the station so we can record your statement. Afterward, you may see your son."

Olli gave one last glance toward the stretcher disappearing down the hall.

Then he nodded.

46

A strange feeling crept over Tuomas—like the one he'd had when the mill elf Jaska had first visited him. Something in the room was off. The hospital was dark, but his sharp night vision allowed him to make out the shadowy figure sitting on the edge of the other bed.

A tall man. Wearing a hat.

Startled, Tuomas jerked upright.

"Don't be afraid, Tomaso," the figure said calmly. "I won't hurt you."

"Who are you? How did you get in here? What do you want?" Tuomas's voice trembled slightly.

"I want to talk to you about the Lava People."

Tuomas blinked. Was this some journalist trying to cash in on a wild story about his miraculous survival? He scowled and switched on the bedside lamp, glaring at the man.

"There's no such thing," he snapped. "Get out of here and let me sleep. I can call the cop outside—he'll be in here in seconds."

"We both know the Lava People exist," the stranger replied, unshaken. "I knew your grandmother."

Tuomas's heart skipped. "But... that was a secret. Nonna never told anyone. Only me."

Instinctively, he reached under his T-shirt, fingers brushing the warm stone on the chain around his neck.

The old man gave a soft, knowing smile. "Take good care of your grandmother's gift."

Tuomas froze. How does he know about the pendant?

He studied the visitor more closely. The man was clearly old—very old—but he didn't seem dangerous. Except for his eyes. They shimmered like sapphires beneath the brim of his hat. His beard glowed auburn in the lamplight, and the hair falling from under the hat was the same vivid red as Tuomas's—or Nonna's.

"Deep down, you know where I come from," the man said. "And you're smart enough to understand what I'm about to tell you."

He paused, voice hoarse, as if unused to speaking aloud.

"The Lava People have no enemies to fear," he began. "As you know, we are invisible to most. Humans are made of matter. We are a form of antimatter. Our energy could wipe out every weapon humans have, destroy cities, end your world."

He paused. His tone softened.

"But we don't want that. We want peace. Still, we face a problem: antimatter cannot regenerate. It cannot reproduce. When one of us turns away from our people, we lose something. Each defector weakens us."

He looked Tuomas directly in the eyes.

"When those traitors bear children with humans, their energy flows into the next generation. That energy belongs to us. And we have the right to reclaim it."

Tuomas's throat tightened.

"Many return their children to us willingly," the man continued. "But some flee, believing they can escape judgment. Your grandmother was one of them."

A long silence stretched between them.

"That's why you're so important," the man said. "You come from a powerful line. The leader's line. You carry strength we cannot afford to lose."

He stood slowly, casting a long shadow across the room.

"But my wife is wrong to think we must force you back. I see things differently. You're old enough to choose. You know what your duty is. Come willingly, and you will live as one of us—immortal, untouchable. Or stay here, and suffer as humans do."

A knock at the door startled them both.

The young policeman popped his head in. "I thought I heard voices."

"I had a bad dream," Tuomas said quickly. "Turned the light on."

"No wonder—dreams like that will mess you up." The officer chuckled. "Don't worry, I'm here all night."

He shut the door again.

The stranger hadn't even flinched. He was invisible to the officer.

Once the door clicked shut, the old man reached into his coat and placed something small and dark on the bedside table.

"There's another way to serve our people," he said. "Many heirs of the Lava People live among humans, unaware of their powers. Some become tyrants. Others lose themselves completely. We call them lost energy."

He gestured to the object.

"This is no ordinary stone. It's a transformer. When it touches a descendant of the Lava People, it draws their power back to us. The person lives on—unchanged in body—but their abilities vanish."

Tuomas stared at him.

"You want me to… take people's powers?"

"Yes. Find those like you. Return the stolen energy. If you succeed, we'll let you live among the humans."

The boy's mind whirled. A hundred questions buzzed inside him. One rose to the surface:

"If I touched you… would the stone take my powers too?"

The old man shook his head.

"Your powers are sealed. Several times over. You're safe."

"Can it… send the energy somewhere else? Not back to the Lava People?"

The old man raised an eyebrow. A faint smile curved his lips.

"You're clever. I expected no less. But I can't answer that. That's for you to discover."

He stepped back into the shadows.

"Remember who you are, Tomaso. The Lava People are your kin. Your task is not to waste what you've been given—but to recover what was lost."

And with that, he was gone.

The stone glinted on the nightstand.

Tuomas stared at it, the pendant warming against his chest.

And he wondered—what would he choose?

"Choose wisely, young prince."

The voice was everywhere and nowhere—echoing in Tuomas's ears, inside his chest, in the very air around him.

"Will you join the human race— that fragile, fleeting species that stumbles through its brief existence, ring the world with greed and ignorance, and returning to dust with nothing to show for its time?"

The voice grew colder, heavier, as if it carried the weight of centuries.

"Or will you choose your true bloodline— the Lava People, ancient as the Earth itself, untouched by death, immune to the rot of time?"

Tuomas felt heat rise beneath his skin. The pendant at his neck pulsed softly, as if it, too, awaited his answer.

"We have walked the surface of the world and its fiery core. We have shaped ourselves into whatever form suits us. We are not bound by the laws of matter. We cannot be destroyed."

The voice softened—seductive now, almost warm.

"You were born of both worlds, but you do not belong to both. You must choose where your loyalty lies. One path offers immortality, power, and purpose. The other… offers suffering, decay, and death."

A final pause.

Then, like molten stone cooling into silence:

"Choose wisely."

The old gentleman raised his hat with a graceful nod.

"It was a pleasure to meet you, my great-great-grandson. We'll meet again, Tommaso."

And just like that—he vanished. Gone, as if he had never been there at all.

Tuomas sat frozen, heart pounding in the quiet hospital room. He took a deep breath and looked around, half-expecting the man to reappear from the shadows.

If what he said is true, Tuomas thought, then Nonna was his daughter. And that means… that man was my great-grandfather.

Not just any great-grandfather, either—the king of the mysterious Lava People.

He rubbed his eyes. Did I dream all that? Or did it really happen?

Then his gaze fell on the object resting on the bedside table.

A stone. Heavy, dark—yet faintly glowing. Tuomas reached for it and held it under the soft light of the bedside lamp. It was warm in his palm, and the glow within it pulsed gently, like embers beneath the surface.

Red like lava.

"Don't forget your origin," the man had said.

Sleep was no longer an option.

Tuomas pulled his tablet from his backpack and began searching for more information about Mount Etna. His thoughts were tangled—part awe, part dread. Somehow, everything that had happened seemed to lead back to that mountain.

Volcanoes had never interested him before. Why would they? In Finland, there were none. No erupting mountains, no mudslides, no hurricanes, no earthquakes. People didn't freeze to death in blizzards anymore. No one suffocated in quicksand or vanished into the sea. Finland was… safe. Predictable.

It wasn't until now that he realized how rare that was.

When the world map of active volcanoes appeared on the screen, Tuomas blinked in disbelief.

Over four thousand.

They came in all kinds—steep, gentle, submerged beneath oceans, collapsed, rising, ancient and quiet, or young and explosive. Some erupted daily, others slept for centuries.

It felt like a miracle that the Earth held together at all, with so much pressure, so much molten fury, just beneath the surface.

He looked up.

Beyond the hospital window, maybe twenty kilometers away, the silhouette of Mount Etna cut a jagged line across the night sky.

It loomed—silent, but alive.

And Tuomas knew.

His story was far from over.

47

The door opened again, and an elderly nurse in a blue coat peeked inside. The hospital was run by a convent, and many of the nurses were nuns—most of them quite old. Their legs looked like thin sticks beneath their calf-length skirts, but they moved through the long corridors with surprising agility, their low heels clicking sharply against the tile floors.

According to convent rules, they wore white headscarves that draped down their backs, tied tightly so that only their faces showed. The nun who entered now wore wire-rimmed glasses, behind which her eyes sparkled kindly.

"I see you still have your light on," she said, settling onto the empty bed beside Tuomas. "Can't sleep, my son?"

She smiled, glancing toward the hallway. "Signore Policeman seems to be snoring in his chair, so I thought I'd check on you."

So much for protection, Tuomas thought. But the nun's presence was strangely comforting. There was something about her that reminded him of Nonna. He glanced at the name tag pinned to the bodice of her habit: Sister Assunta.

"You've had a busy day," she said, watching him gently.

"Yes…" Tuomas replied quietly.

"You were very lucky," she said. "Not everyone who falls into a volcano lives to tell the tale. The old stories say the volcano gods don't take kindly to strangers."

Tuomas hesitated. "You're… quite old, Signora. I mean."

"Old enough to know things," she interrupted, smiling. "Things most people wouldn't believe. I imagine that's what you meant."

He nodded slowly.

"I'd like to hear more about the volcano," he said. "I can't sleep anyway."

"I could tell you a Sicilian bedtime story, then," she said with a wink. "But you mustn't tell anyone I told it to you."

Tuomas leaned in.

"They say invisible beings live inside the volcanoes," Sister Assunta began, her voice low and rhythmic. "Sometimes they come to the surface in human form. It's said that when a girl is tending sheep on the slopes, a stranger might appear—tall, handsome, and glowing with warmth. They fall in love... or at least, well... certain things happen."

She gave Tuomas a wry smile.

"And then," she continued, "a very special child is born."

Tuomas's mouth went dry. "How do you know that?"

The nun paused for a moment, then said, "If a child is born with red hair, people here say it might be a Vulcan child. Not always, of course. But redheads are watched closely. Feared. Some have bad luck. Others... disappear."

"Disappear?" Tuomas echoed, horrified.

"There are rumors," she said softly. "Some mothers—terrified of what they'd given birth to—took their children to the volcano, where... they were collected."

Tuomas's face went pale. "But they were just children!"

"Some mothers even tried to jump in with them," Sister Assunta added. "But they weren't permitted to enter. Their bodies were found later—on the outer slopes, untouched by lava."

Tuomas shook his head. "How can people be so cruel?"

"Fear makes monsters of good people," the nun said. "But there were also mothers who stood by their red-haired children. Who fled into the countryside. Some of those children survived. They grew… different. Some used their gifts for selfish things. A few, for good."

Tuomas stared at her, then asked, "How do you know all this, Sister Assunta? These stories… they're secrets."

The nun hesitated. Then, slowly, she reached up and removed the headband from her headscarf, letting it fall to her shoulders.

A thick knot of hair came loose. It was bright red—like fire under moonlight.

She removed her glasses. Her eyes, now unhidden, were sapphire blue.

The same as Tuomas's.

The same as Nonna's.

For a long moment, neither spoke.

Then Sister Assunta tied her scarf back in place and slipped her glasses on.

"You're wondering how I survived," she said. "My mother hid me in this convent when I was still small. The nuns didn't believe in volcano spirits—they believed in God. And in God's house, I was safe."

"You stayed here your whole life?"

"I became one of them," she said with a soft smile. "I still am. Because I've remained… pure, like the Virgin Mary, the Lava People cannot take me. Not yet. When I die, they'll try. But until then, I live among humans, in peace."

Tuomas leaned closer. "Do you have powers too?"

"Yes," she admitted. "But I rarely use them. And when I do, I give the credit to God. It's safer that way. Easier."

She looked at him seriously.

"You should do the same. Keep your gifts quiet. Live as normal a life as you can. The fire inside us—it burns. It pushes us to do more. To be more. But some can't handle the weight. Many end up addicted. Lost. Some... don't survive."

Tuomas swallowed hard.

Then he asked the question that had haunted him since he first heard about the Lava People: "How do you think they live?"

Sister Assunta grew quiet.

"No one knows," she said at last. "Because no one who's gone back has ever returned. If I'm honest... I'm afraid of it. Afraid of going back. I'd rather be buried behind the convent wall, under the jasmine and the roses, like all the other sisters."

As she spoke, she reached for the glowing stone on Tuomas's bedside table—the one left by the Lava King— and gently ran her fingers across its surface.

"But now," she said softly, "you really must sleep."

She placed the stone back on the table, rose with a quiet sigh, and leaned over him. She kissed his forehead tenderly, took the tablet from his hands, and placed it on the other bed. Then she straightened her habit, pulling the headgear tight, careful to cover every strand of hair.

But what she didn't notice—what Tuomas did—was that her once bright hair had turned silver-gray.

Her sapphire eyes had dulled to gray as well.

The stone had taken her powers. She no longer belonged to the Lava People.

No one could force her to return.

She left the room without another word.

Tuomas rose from bed, pulled his backpack from the closet, and rummaged until he found a pair of old socks. He carefully wrapped the glowing stone in one and tucked it deep into the bottom of the pack.

From the hallway came the loud snore of the dozing policeman.

But Tuomas felt calm now. Sister Assunta was still watching over the hospital.

And within moments, he slipped into a deep, dreamless sleep.

48

The next morning, Tuomas was awakened by a new nun. Sister Assunta's shift, it seemed, had ended. The nurse checked his blood pressure and pulse, then gave a satisfied nod.

"Everything looks good," she said, placing a tray in front of him. "Breakfast."

Tuomas blinked at the simple but comforting meal—fresh rolls with honey and a glass of juice. For the first time in days, things seemed to be returning to normal.

Around eight o'clock, the door opened again. This time, the doctor entered, followed by another nun and three men: an inspector, a psychologist, and—most importantly—his father.

Olli gave him a quick, reassuring smile but didn't rush forward. The doctor asked the group to wait outside while he performed one last exam.

He reviewed the nurse's notes, then gently checked Tuomas's eyes with a penlight and listened to his breathing through the stethoscope.

"Well, young man," he said, lowering the device, "how do you feel today?"

Tuomas shrugged. "Same as yesterday. I feel fine."

"Do you remember what happened yesterday?"

Tuomas gave a small, sly smile. "It was… adventurous. I've never jumped with a parachute before."

The doctor chuckled. "You didn't break any bones, which is remarkable. But there may have been a slight concussion—it could affect your memory a bit."

Tuomas gave another shrug.

"The police would like to ask you a few questions. Do you feel up to it?"

"Can I go home with my father afterward?"

"If the police agree."

The doctor stepped aside and opened the door. The three men entered.

Olli was the first to reach him, pulling him into a quick, relieved hug. In one hand he held a newspaper, folded in half. Tuomas caught a glimpse of the headline and his own photo under it.

"You're a hero," his father said, shaking his head in amazement.

"You're the real hero," Tuomas replied quietly. "You saved all those people."

Before Olli could respond, the inspector stepped forward.

"Tuomas," he said gently, "can you describe the man who grabbed you on the plane? Had you seen him before?"

Tuomas shook his head. "No. He was completely crazy."

"Do you remember where you landed?"

Tuomas hesitated. How could he explain what had happened without revealing the truth? He pictured the glowing crater, the parachute, the man disappearing into the fumes.

"I think… he let go of me just before we hit the ground. I landed on my own. I don't really remember the rest."

"I see." The inspector jotted a few notes. "If we find him, would you be able to identify him—maybe over Skype?"

"Sure. If you catch him."

Olli stepped in. "If there's nothing else, I'd like to take my son home. We're heading back to Finland today."

The inspector gave a slow nod. "From my point of view, there's no reason to hold him. You're free to go."

Tuomas exhaled, finally allowing himself to relax. Sicily, for all its heat and mystery, would soon be nothing more than a memory—one he wasn't sure he wanted to revisit.

A few days later, Sicilian police received a curious report.

A man had been found at dawn, sitting naked on the steps of a small tourist bar high on the slopes of Mount Etna. His face was swollen and bruised beyond recognition—his own mother wouldn't have known him. He didn't speak. Not Italian. Not English. Not anything. No ID, no passport, no fingerprints in any database.

The working theory was simple: a tourist who had been drugged and robbed.

Until someone claimed him, he was sent to a locked psychiatric ward, where he sat quietly, staring into nothing.

No one noticed the faint smell of smoke that lingered on him. Or the faint shimmer of heat in his eyes.

No one asked what he had seen.

No one asked what he had lost.

49

The return trip to Finland was uneventful. Tuomas and his father were guided through secure staff-only corridors and became the last passengers to board the flight. This allowed them to avoid the cameras and the barrage of questions from paparazzi waiting in the terminal. Sensational headlines about the heroic pilot and the miraculous survival of his son had already begun circulating in the media. A few passengers from the hijacked flight had given interviews, embellishing what little they knew.

Fortunately, the bizarre "air war" between airport security and the rogue seagull hadn't made it into the papers. No one had been injured. No planes had been damaged. The story was quietly forgotten.

Once onboard, the airline staff ushered Tuomas and his father to the first row of first class. As the engines roared and the plane lifted into the sky, Tuomas leaned against the window, watching the smoking silhouette of Mount Etna shrink into the haze below.

Something twisted in his chest.

Was that where I belong?

Is that my home? My people?

He didn't want it to be true.

He reached for his father's hand and squeezed it tightly.

"Don't worry," Olli said gently, sensing his son's unease. "I heard there are four civilian security guards on board. We'll be home soon. Everything will be fine."

If only that were true, Tuomas thought.

But nothing felt fine.

Nonna was gone.

His ancestors, if they were even real, belonged to another world—one born of flame and shadow. A place that whispered to him from beneath the earth.

And now that world wanted him back.

The Lava People. The ones who called him heir. Who tried to take him into the depths of the volcano.

He didn't even know who he was anymore.

Worst of all, he feared himself. What was growing inside him? What had already awakened? Was he a danger—like a sleeping bomb, waiting to go off? Could he hurt someone without meaning to?

There was no one to guide him. No teacher. No manual. Just a glowing stone wrapped in a sock at the bottom of his backpack—and a heart full of questions.

Who would believe him, anyway?

The more he thought about it, the more unreal it all seemed. The fire, the fall, the flight. The voices in the night.

Maybe it was all just… a story.

He remembered what Sister Assunta had told him that night in the hospital:

"It's easier to live as an ordinary person."

And maybe it was.

Tuomas closed his eyes and rested his head on his father's shoulder.

For now, he would try. He would try to be just a boy. A regular boy. He would do his best to live a normal life.

Even if part of him would always burn quietly beneath the surface.

END OF THE 1ST BAND

Continue reading now:
Volume 2: The Lava Prince and the Magic Stone

Places

ARVOLA (name changed) is a seaside settlement of several thousand inhabitants that lost many of its public facilities after forced incorporation.

Arko Manor (name changed) is a historical manor house in the village of Arvola. Located at the intersection of the road and the waterway, it was a famous coach station at the end of the 19th century.

People

Tuomas Arkko: a half-orphan and schoolboy who becomes aware of his supernatural powers as he grows older. The origin of these powers is explained to him by his Sicilian grandmother on her deathbed. "Am I even human?" Tuomas often asks himself.

Olli Arkko: Tuomas' father, a commercial pilot by profession, is forced to take his son from Helsinki to live with his grandmother at the family estate, Arko Manor, after the death of his mother.

Angela Arkko (née Costa): Tuomas' Italian mother, who dies together with her brother Carlo Costa in a car accident.

Irma Arkko: The mistress of the Arkko estate and Tuomas' grandmother, who wants nothing to do with her role as a grandmother.

Alma: the long-time housekeeper of the Arkko estate and Tuomas' motherly support.

Jaska: the centuries-old mill elf of the Arkko estate, who becomes a good friend of Tuomas.

Tuomas' Italian family:

Olivia: After the great eruption of Mount Etna in the 1920s, Sicilian Maurizio Costa meets and marries the mysterious, beautiful, red-haired Olivia. Only on her deathbed does Nonna Olivia (nonna = Italian for grandmother) dare to reveal to her grandson that she, like Tuomas, belongs to the invisible lava people.

Carlo Costa: Angela's brother and Tuomas' uncle.

Sofia Costa: Wife of Carlo Costa and mother of Chiara, Tuomas' cousin. Sofia runs the restaurant La Colombaia since the death of her husband.

Chiara Costa: Italian cousin of Tuomas.

Volume 2:

The Lava Prince and the Magic Stone

T uomas' extraordinary supernatural abilities lead him into a series of adventures. He gradually learns to use the powers he inherited from the Lava People wisely and always for the good of humanity. Immediately upon his return, he rescues puppies from the clutches of illegal traders.

Back in the village of Arvola, he witnesses a robbery at the local grocery store and plays a not-insignificant role in an exciting event surrounding the old windmill. The village's dilapidated wooden church is also the scene of mysterious tales of ghosts and robbers - and of course, Tuomas and his powers are right in the middle of it all, as he fights to preserve the historic building.

As a descendant of the Lava People, Tuomas has a special relationship with fire and eventually joins the local volunteer fire department.

But he is also confronted with the challenges of migrants and begins to get involved in environmental activities, led by the courageous Saga from Sweden. With his special abilities, he actively supports her - even a powerful president can't stop him.

The words of the Lava King echo in his head: "**Choose wisely, young prince...**".

About the Author

Leena-Marjatta Pulfer-Korhonen was born in the Finnish village of Otava on February 10, 1942. After graduating from a girls' high school in Mikkeli, Leena studied Finnish language and literature at the University of Helsinki, graduating with a master's degree in philosophy. In 1969 she married the journalist Fritz Pulfer in Zurich. From then on Leena lived in Switzerland.

At the end of a busy period, the couple moved back to Finland, to Leena's home village of Otava. Here she found the leisure and time to devote to her favorite pastime, writing. She finished the imaginative story of the lava prince Tuomas. The two books are Leena's gift to her home community, because in them she was able to realize many things that the present suburb of Mikkeli.

Leena was able to finish her work. Unfortunately, an incurable cancer prevented her from holding the printed books in her hands. Leena died on June 17th, 2023.